The Ninth Inning
Three Rivers Ranch Romance™
Book 8

Liz Isaacson

Copyright © 2023 by Elana Johnson, writing as Liz Isaacson

All rights reserved.

No part of this book may be reproduced in any form or by any electronic or mechanical means, including information storage and retrieval systems, without written permission from the author, except for the use of brief quotations in a book review.

ISBN-13: 978-1-63876-289-8

"Blessed is that man that maketh the Lord his trust, and respecteth not the proud, nor such as turn aside to lies."

Psalms 40:4

Chapter One

Sundays had never felt so problematic for Andrea Larsen. Of course, she'd been enjoying her day of rest for years, sitting by her mother at church, attending the picnic, and basking in the one day off she had each week.

Now, with Mama gone, Andy sat alone during the sermon, didn't like lingering afterward, and escaped inside her boutique just to pass the hours until Monday.

Today, she unpackaged a new shipment of blouses perfect for the upcoming holiday season while the winter wind in Texas tried to get in through the shop window's cracks.

She nursed a mug of hot chocolate, her mind far away—at Three Rivers Ranch, where Lawrence Collins worked. She couldn't help thinking about him during the Thanksgiving season, as that's when she'd broken up with him. But now, the tall, sandy-haired, bright blue-eyed cowboy dominated her thoughts.

Regret lanced through her heart, and once again, she contemplated calling him and apologizing. After all, she'd been wrong. He hadn't been dating another woman in Amarillo, but going there to visit his younger sister who'd gotten pregnant and was afraid to tell her parents.

As quickly as the remorse had settled, her pride pushed it out. She could never tell him she'd been wrong, though in the quiet moments—like today—she fantasized about what life would be like if she could muster the courage to apologize.

Would he forgive her?

Could they start over?

Her phone chimed, a peculiar sound for a notification she didn't recognize. At least it drove Lawrence from her mind. When she checked her device, she saw she'd received her first online order. Her brand spanking new system had just been implemented a month ago in anticipation of the holiday season, and a brief balloon of joy lifted her spirits.

Carly Sanders apparently needed a new black pencil skirt and a blouse in "green, white, and black."

Andy didn't stock everything, but she *had* just gotten in a selection of items in holiday colors—

The Ninth Inning

including green. She turned on her Internet radio as she browsed her boutique, some of the disquiet of this lonely Sunday drifting into the rafters.

Monday morning, before she usually left the loft above her shop, Andy armed herself with Carly's purchases and set her car on the road. Almost an afterthought, she checked the delivery address.

Her stomach fell to her shoes when she saw she needed to drive all the way out to Three Rivers Ranch. A river of trepidation wound through Andy, mostly because the possibility of seeing Lawrence existed. Of course, she'd seen him at church and around town—it was a small place, after all. But she'd managed to put people between them and keep their paths from fully crossing.

Embarrassment ran with the anxiety. She really just needed to clear the air between them. Then she wouldn't have to worry about seeing him at the grocery store, or the picnic—or the ranch.

She dialed Carly. "You want these clothes out at Three Rivers?"

Scuffling came through the line. "You've got them already?"

"Yeah, I just got a new shipment of holiday things over the weekend. You're going to love the blouse I picked out for you. The stripes are fantastic and will look great on you."

"That's great." But Carly didn't sound like it was great. She seemed distracted.

"I was heading over to your place now." Andy watched a pair of boys walk in front of her, clearly on their way to school. "But then I realized you set the delivery address to the ranch. Have you left for work yet?"

"Yeah. Yes, I'm here." A door slammed on Carly's end of the line. "I want to model the clothes for…uh, a Christmas party we're having here at Courage Reins. That's why I need them out here." Murmurs came through the line, and Carly said, "I know," to someone else.

"Is that okay?" she asked Andy. "If you can't make it here and back by the time you need to open, you could come tomorrow."

Andy frowned. If Carly didn't need the clothes until tomorrow…. She shook her head. She was up, already sitting in the car. "I'm on my way." Even driving eighty minutes round-trip was better than puttering around the shop. Again.

Carly emitted a tiny squeak before she hung up. Andy swung through a drive-through for a cup of coffee and set her car north. The gray skies complimented her mood as she drove.

She usually enjoyed the quiet, quaint atmosphere of Three Rivers. But she felt unsettled now that Mama

The Ninth Inning

had died. Now that she was all alone. Just her and her building now. She hadn't had much romantic luck after Lawrence.

"Maybe because you compare every man to him," she muttered to herself as she tried to take some measure of calmness from the beauty of the landscape. The blowing trees only satisfied her soul for a moment. Then she felt like those trees, being whipped and pushed whichever way the wind happened to blow.

Andy didn't want to be ungrounded. Not anymore. She wanted to take control of her life, the way she had her business. She turned onto the dirt road leading to the ranch, a swift gust of wind knocking into her car. Tightening her grip on the wheel, she glanced into the sky and watched the swirling storm.

She urged her car to go a bit faster on the bumpy road, hoping to make it inside the building before the skies opened. Her teeth knocked together as she rounded the last corner. A new building, nearly complete, sat just on the corner, with fenced in arenas and another barn.

A dark haired woman Andy had seen a couple of times at church pushed her whole weight against a barrel, inching it along the dirt. She dusted off her hands and glanced at the sky, then at Andy as she passed.

She raised her hand in a friendly greeting, and

Andy struggled to recall her name. She hadn't come into the boutique before, and she'd rented the old Johnson house that had been empty for years.

"Brynn," Andy said, proud of herself for remembering that much. She'd heard Brynn was starting a horse training facility at the ranch, and it looked like the rumors held truth.

Thunder rumbled the sky, and Andy focused. But the paved parking lot in front of the Courage Reins administration building was full.

Full.

She bypassed it, lightning flashing against the front windows of the building, and pulled down the lane where a variety of ranch vehicles crowded together. One space remained, and she swung into it and grabbed the bag containing Carly's new clothes from the passenger seat.

She'd opened her door and stood when the deluge of rain came. Yelping, she cradled the bag in her arms and ran for the closest building to wait out the downpour.

Her shoes ate up the few yards to the horse barn, but they couldn't escape the water. By the time she found refuge, mud had splattered her ballet flats and splashed up the calves of her slacks. At least the clothes were dry. Mostly.

"Wet out there." The man spoke so quietly, Andy

The Ninth Inning

barely heard him. At least with her ears. That voice, though, was ingrained in her mind, buried deep in her heart. Had been since she met him at the rodeo and been charmed by his subtle strength. Had been for six months while they dated.

She turned as if in slow motion toward Lawrence, who stood a few paces away in all his glory. Black cowboy hat. Dark leather jacket. Jeans that stretched down his long legs to his boots. Her eyes traveled back to his before her vocal cords remembered how to work.

If only she could think of something to say. Her brain threw suggestions at her: *Hey.* Or maybe *Good morning.* Even *How's everything?* would've worked.

Nothing came out of her mouth.

"You look great," he said, taking a careful step closer.

"Thank you," misted from her mouth, though nothing about her looked great. But she'd always been polite, even when confronted with difficult situations. One sweep of Lawrence, and she knew she'd hurt him badly. Unintentionally, but the breakup still sliced at her every time she thought of it, and she hadn't been wrongly accused.

He kept coming forward, stopping only a few feet from her, and leaned against the railing. "Those Miss Carly's clothes?"

Andy dropped the bag like it was crime scene

evidence and she didn't want to be seen with it. She combed her fingers through her sopping hair, wishing she didn't look and feel like a drowned rat.

He bent to pick up the bag. "Looks like 'em." He glanced at her. "You've lost your voice or something?"

Andy blinked and then pressed her eyes closed for a long moment. "Good morning, Lawrence."

He grinned, that sexy, soft smile she'd fallen in love with the first time she'd seen it. Her heart hammered against her breastbone.

"Mornin' to you too, Miss Andy." He stepped forward—again—and handed her the bag. She took it with numb fingers and waited for him to fall back against the rail. He didn't.

He swept his hand down the side of her face. "I miss you."

Her throat squeezed. Squeezed against the emotion in his voice. Squeezed against her own desire and longing to be with Lawrence again. Squeezed against the apology crowding her chest.

"It's good to see you again," she managed to say. Her arms itched to wrap themselves around him and hold on tight. Her feet urged her to leave, and leave now. The rain pounded the ground outside the barn, and she couldn't escape. She peered into the atmosphere, wishing she could.

"Andy—" Lawrence started.

The Ninth Inning

"I'm sorry," she blurted. "Okay? I'm sorry I accused you of cheating on me." Andy looked up, right into his dazzling blue eyes. "I was wrong."

His eyes blazed, first with heat, then with forgiveness, and finally with happiness. "Yeah, you were." He sighed. "But at least now I don't have to ask Miss Carly to lie for me again."

As lost as Andy felt inside his gaze, she still comprehended his words. "What?"

"She didn't order those clothes."

"She didn't?" Andy realized she'd been leaning forward, and she righted herself before she did something she couldn't undo.

"I did," Lawrence said. "Wanted to get you out to the ranch so we could talk."

Andy didn't know what to say, what he could possibly want to talk about. She glared at him, conversation topics they used to enjoy completely off-limits.

Despite the way her mind whirred, trying to think through what he needed to say, the heavy load she'd been carrying for the past year dissipated, eased from her shoulders.

Thank you, Lord, she thought, *for giving me the courage to apologize and for allowing Lawrence to accept it.*

He paced away from her, and a blip of fear stole through her. He had forgiven her, hadn't he?

* * *

Lawrence moved away from Andy, the intoxicating scent of her beachy perfume overwhelming his rationality. Plus, after he'd told her that he'd lured her out to the ranch with an online order from her boutique, she carried a violent edge in her eye, and Lawrence liked his nose whole, thank you very much.

"You can be mad," he said. "But I was tired of avoiding you at church and in town."

"All those cars in the parking lot...."

Lawrence turned and leaned against a post, a healthy distance from her. He kicked a smile in her direction. "You'd be surprised how long it takes to get enough people to move their vehicles." Especially because they all wanted an explanation. Thankfully, Carly could charm a cat to give up its catch, and she'd been able to fill the parking lot before Andy arrived. Barely.

"So you left me that one spot." Andy gestured toward the door, where the rain still fell. "Did you order up the rain too?"

"No, that was just lucky."

She cocked her hip and folded her arms, and Lawrence wished the sight of her didn't drive his pulse into overdrive. He watched her as her mind bent

The Ninth Inning

around his set-up. So much of Andy was reactionary—like the first time they'd met and she'd slid her hand into his during the barrel racing—but she also had a side of her that took time to process. Time to think through what she should say.

"Well, now what?" she asked, smoothing down her festive crimson sweater. She'd paired it with a pair of black slacks, which hugged her petite frame, and a pair of ballet flats, which bore the muddy evidence of her escape into the barn.

"Now nothing," Lawrence said, though a dinner invitation sat on the tip of his tongue. "I just wanted to see you and tell you I'm not upset with you." He wanted more than that, but he buried the words deep. Couldn't speak them too soon.

She combed her fingers through her coffee-colored hair and trained her tea-colored eyes on him. He'd lost himself to her beauty before, and he felt himself falling again. He glanced away.

"Sorry about your momma," he said.

She inhaled sharply, sending a hiss through the barn. "You came to the funeral. You already paid your respects."

"Not to you." He stuffed his hands in his pockets as they tingled in anticipation of holding hers. "You doin' okay?"

"Fine."

Which meant no. He wondered if she'd holed herself up in her loft, lost herself in her boutique, spent too much money and too many hours shopping online. One look at Andy, and he knew she'd done all of that.

"What are you doin' for Thanksgiving?" he asked.

"Baking pumpkin pie and roasting a turkey."

"For one?"

She lifted her chin. "Yes."

"You shouldn't do that." He couldn't stop himself from moving a little closer. Maybe not within arm's reach, but near enough to smell that blasted perfume. "Come on out here. Kelly and Chelsea are preparing a feast fit for kings." He nodded to the bag of clothes she still held. "Carly will probably need to order a bigger size after what they have planned." He chuckled. "Don't you tell her I said that, though."

A ghost of a smile crossed her face. "It'll be our little secret."

Surprise jolted through him at the familiar words. A game they used to play during the months they'd dated.

"Don't tell anyone I let you in my storeroom." She gives him a flirtatious grin as she pushes open the door. "I never let anyone in here, not even Mama."

"It'll be our little secret," he tells her as he enters, pulls her with him, and closes the door. He kisses her in

The Ninth Inning

the privacy of her storeroom, away from the window shopping ladies on the sidewalk. Their little secret.

Lawrence shook the memories from his head, but the fantasy that he and Andy could play such games again remained in full force.

She seemed to remember what the words represented, and her face turned to stone. "I can't come for Thanksgiving." She spun and faced the weather.

He joined her at her side. "Of course you can. You have nowhere else to go." He put his hand on her arm for barely a breath. There, then gone. "You shouldn't be alone at the holidays."

"Will you go home to Amarillo?"

"Not this year." He focused on the rain too, watched the wind drive it sideways. "My folks are goin' on a cruise. I'm staying here. Maybe I'll even help with the baking."

Andy gave him the response he wanted—she threw her head back and laughed. "I'll eat before I come out, then."

"Hey, who says I haven't improved since last year?"

She tossed him a smirk. "Have you?"

"Not even a little bit." He nudged her side. "Does that mean you'll come?" He didn't dare to hope, yet the feeling swelled inside him, expanding until it filled his whole body.

She drew the silence into long ribbons, until the

unease inside Lawrence threatened to tear him apart. He hadn't dated anyone since Andy. He couldn't. He believed her to be the only one for him.

Now he just needed her to believe it too.

He tilted his head toward the barn's rafters. *How do I make her believe it too?*

He'd been asking God the same question for months, and finally he'd had the idea to use her online shopping service to get her to talk to him. But now he didn't know what else to say, and the Lord was silent on the matter as well.

Chapter Two

Andy drank in the warmth from Lawrence's body, inhaled the spicy scent of his aftershave and the comforting smell of leather and horse that accompanied him everywhere. Something about leaning her head against his shoulder would be natural, but a layer of awkwardness existed between them as well.

"You still have my number?" His question shattered the ice between them.

Her stomach squirmed. What would he think if she said no? What would it imply if she said yes?

She decided to be truthful. "Yes."

"Great," he said, his tone unreadable. "Text me and let me know what you decide." He flipped up the collar of his jacket, took the bag from her hand, and stepped into the downpour. "By this weekend would be nice," he called over his shoulder as the rain concealed him in misty grayness.

A keen sense of loss accompanied his absence, and Andy struggled to make sense of it. In the end, she turned back to the barn, reasoning away her feelings as a side effect of her lingering loneliness. She just missed her mother. Missed having days where the world felt right, like things made sense.

Because nothing right now made sense. Lawrence shouldn't have lured her out here. He shouldn't be so happy to see her. He should be upset with her. The fact that he wasn't ignited a fire in her belly she didn't know what to do with.

She wandered down the aisle in the barn, a bit startled when a horse nosed her on her way by. "Hey, there." She stroked her hand down his nearly black cheeks, pleased with the serenity of the animal, the lazy way he closed his eyes halfway.

The alarm on her phone went off, and Andy headed toward the exit. She knew she'd sit and visit with Carly, and she'd set the alarm to let her know when she needed to leave so she could get back to the boutique and open on time.

The rain had let up a little bit—not enough to go traipsing around in, but enough for her to tiptoe-run to her car without much more damage to her shoes and slacks.

The Ninth Inning

The damage to her heart, however, seemed to multiply as she drove by the packed parking lot and found Lawrence leaning against one of the trucks, the rain dripping off his cowboy hat, watching her.

THE WEEK PASSED, with one day blending into another. Andy swept her store, played lilting music, sold a handful of dresses to a few people. She expected a rush next week before Thanksgiving, and of course, on Black Friday. But the calm before the storm brought nothing but mind-numbing boredom.

She used to play games on her phone, but having the device so close—with Lawrence's number still programmed in and his invitation to Thanksgiving dinner ringing loudly in her ears—had proven dangerous.

She'd had an acceptance text all typed out before she realized what it could mean. Or maybe it wouldn't mean anything. Maybe she just didn't want to roast her own turkey. Maybe spending time with a big group was just what she needed to get out of the slump she'd fallen into since she broke up with Lawrence and then lost her mother.

On Friday afternoon, the bell on her door tinkled,

bringing her attention from the fashion magazine spread before her. A smile bounced to her face.

"Carly, hey."

"Okay, so you're not mad at me." The blonde woman strode toward her as best as she could in her high heels. "Because you haven't called, or demanded payment for the clothes, or texted Lawrence about Thanksgiving."

Andy moved around the counter at the same time Carly arrived, and she embraced her friend. "I'm not mad." She stepped back. "But I do need you to pay for the clothes." She glanced at what Carly wore. "Oh, they look great on you. Spin."

Carly obliged, and satisfaction slipped through Andy at the exact fit of the skirt, the way the black and white stripes—with a green one every third line—slimmed Carly at the waist.

Her friend pulled out her debit card. "So about Thanksgiving...."

"I'm still thinking about it." Andy started the transaction as a way to keep her hands and eyes busy.

"It's just one dinner," Carly said. "There will be loads of people there. Kelly invited her parents. Kate and Brett are here from North Carolina while he builds Brynn Bowman's facility." Carly frowned faintly. "But I think they're going to Oklahoma City to visit his family. But there will still be lots of people there."

"Sure," Andy said, sliding the receipt across the counter. "So it's not like Lawrence and I will be on a date." She leaned her elbows on the counter. "But everyone *will* be staring at us. Wondering. Rumors will fly afterward." This was Three Rivers, after all. Large enough to not know everyone, but small enough that everyone seemed to hear about everyone else's business.

"Who cares if they do?" Carly pushed the signed receipt back. "It's Thanksgiving." She put her hand on Andy's. "Your first one without your mom. Come hang out with me. Just don't stay here by yourself."

The barriers Andy kept employed around customers, around everyone, crumbled. She dropped her eyes to the counter, the cracks in her heart spreading as she let the hurt inside.

"Okay," she said.

Carly squealed and tucked her card back into her wallet. "Okay, now text Lawrence and let him know. I promised him I wouldn't badger you about coming."

Andy's gaze flew to her friend's. "But you *are* badgering me about coming."

"Shh." Carly grinned. "Don't tell him I stopped by." She pulled on Andy's hand until she moved around the counter. Carly tucked her elbow in Andy's as they strolled toward the door. "You should see the poor guy. He's moping all over the place, shooting dark glares at Reese like it's his fault you haven't texted. He eats lunch with me everyday. Just sits there, eating silently. At the end, when he gets up, he says, 'Do you think she'll come?' It's sad."

Honey flowed through Andy's veins as she listened to Carly tell her about Lawrence's behavior. "What do you tell him when he asks?"

"I tell him I'm sure you'll come. That you don't really want to be alone, here in your loft, with a turkey dinner for one." They reached the door, and Carly dropped Andy's arm. "Now don't make a liar out of me."

Andy promised Carly she wouldn't, said goodbye, and returned to the counter. She'd left her phone upstairs in her loft and the shop wasn't set to close for another hour. She glanced toward the boutique's entrance, then to the stairs leading to her loft.

She strode toward the door, flipped the open sign to closed and dashed up the steps to retrieve her cell, knowing if she waited, she'd talk herself out of texting Lawrence, out of closing early, out of going to Thanksgiving dinner completely.

The Ninth Inning

LAWRENCE'S PHONE went off at the exact moment Gwen walked into the barn. Frustrated and curious and unwilling to get in trouble for texting while with a client, he didn't remove it from his pocket.

He hugged Gwen instead, glad he'd made the right choice as Pete started across the road. "Hey, Gwen," he said. "After you ride, Reese wants to see you in the office. I guess Carly found something you can put on your medical forms."

"Sure thing." She smiled at him. Pete tipped his hat to them both and continued through the barn and into the outdoor arena, where another client rode.

Lawrence took Gwen to the tack room. "Who do you want today?"

"Who needs the exercise?" She pulled down a saddle and gathered a blanket from the cabinet.

"Raven hasn't been ridden yet today. Neither has Hank. Or you could go with Chocolate. I know you like him."

She chuckled and finished collecting her supplies. "I do like Chocolate."

"Chocolate it is." Lawrence waited for her to go first, his first instinct to reach for his phone and just see if Andy had texted. He chastised himself for even thinking it could be her. She hadn't messaged once this week, though she'd admitted she still had his number. He couldn't lie; knowing she hadn't deleted his number from her phone when she'd removed him from her life had made him happier than he'd been in months.

It meant he still had a chance.

Her days of silence spoke a different story, but Lawrence refused to listen to it.

He couldn't take another moment of not knowing who'd texted. As Gwen saddled Chocolate, Lawrence pulled his phone from his back pocket. A quick swipe, a fast glance.

Andy.

His heart softened into a puddle as a grin graced his face. She'd texted. He stuffed his phone back in his pocket. He could wait an hour to see what she said. At least she'd texted.

Coaching Gwen through what to do became easy after he'd checked his phone. He found he could think about something besides Andy, besides stalking into Carly's office and silently begging her to reassure him he hadn't ruined any and every chance with Andy by ordering those clothes.

He enjoyed his time in the arena for the first time in a week. Gwen accompanied him back to the building, where Reese sat with his head bent over something at his desk.

"Carly said she had something for Miss Gwen," Lawrence said.

Reese glanced up, his eyes glazed. He blinked.

The Ninth Inning

"Oh, yeah." He shuffled some papers around on the desk. "She said your insurance company was giving you trouble about the sessions. She said this code should cover it."

Gwen took the papers with a smile. "Thanks. Is she here?"

"No, she had to run into town for a few minutes." Reese glanced at Lawrence, which caused his throat to tighten. Carly had gone to town?

And Andy had texted.

Lawrence clenched his jaw, determined to keep his comments to himself until Gwen had left.

"Well, tell her thanks for me." Gwen said before she limped toward the exit.

"There's a number on there," Reese called after her. "If they give you any trouble, Carly said to give them that number."

Gwen paused at the door, peering at the papers. "Great. Thanks, Reese." She pushed out the door, and Lawrence waited until it settled closed.

"She went to talk to Andy, didn't she?" he asked Reese.

The cowboy blinked. "I don't exactly know." He slid back in his seat, his expression neutral.

Lawrence appreciated Reese, had always liked him. "I know she did. She promised me she wouldn't."

"Sometimes women just need an extra push,"

Reese said, standing and stretching his back. "Who didn't get ridden today? I have to wait for Carly to come back, and I can't stand bein' at this desk for another second." He studied Lawrence. "You wanna join me?"

"Raven and Hank." Lawrence looked out of the front of the building, made entirely of windows. "And a horseback ride sounds great. Can we get out of the arena, though? Maybe go out on the range a ways?"

"Not far," Reese said. "I'm tired. It's been a busy week."

"No, not far," Lawrence agreed. But he wanted to go really far. Maybe far enough to escape everyone and figure out what to do next. "I'll meet you over there." He pulled out his phone to properly read Andy's text.

Lawrence, it's Andy. I'd like to come to Thanksgiving dinner out at the ranch, if the invitation is still available.

Smiling because she felt like she needed to identify herself—as if he'd purged her number from his phone—he tapped out a response. *It's still available. Chelsea is hosting this year.*

He wanted to add so much more, but he stilled his fingers and waited for her to text back. When she didn't, he sent, *Lunch will be served at 1 pm on Thanksgiving Day. You can come anytime that morning. Stay as late as you want.*

The Ninth Inning

He gave her a few more seconds, then stuffed his phone in his back pocket and headed out to the horse barn. Maybe if he rode far enough, he'd be out of cell phone range and he wouldn't have to obsessively check his messages. But he'd never get her sweet voice telling him she was wrong out of his head.

Chapter Three

Andy changed her clothes at least four times on Thanksgiving Day, unsure of what one wore to a dinner party.

"It's not a dinner party," she told herself as she headed downstairs to find something from the boutique. "It's lunch on a ranch. Black tie is not necessary."

She wanted to look cute, but casual. Friendly, but not flirty. Touchable, but textured. She pushed hangers holding sweaters and jackets to the side, searching for the right thing. She was sure she'd seen it come through the storeroom, she just didn't know what it was. Yet.

Andy glanced toward where she kept the extra inventory, remembering the first time she'd let Lawrence come back there with her. Her hand drifted toward her lips, lightly touching them before shaking herself out of the trance and focusing back on the clothing racks.

Her eyes caught the black and white striped blouse with the third green stripe. She called Carly. "What are you wearing to lunch today?"

Carly laughed. "Oh, girl. Are you that worried about it?"

Andy fingered the silky cotton. "No," she scoffed though her insides were rioting. "I was thinking of wearing that blouse you bought. Don't want to be twinsies though."

"I'm not wearing that."

"What are you wearing?"

"Jeans and that brick red peasant shirt you sold me last month."

"I've never seen you actually wear jeans." Andy paused in her clothing perusal and cocked her head to the side, as if she could detect Carly's lie that way.

"They're denim," she defended.

"Jeggings? That peasant shirt was really long, wasn't it?"

"Yes, okay. There're jeggings." A beat of silence passed. "Am I too old for jeggings?"

Andy laughed. "No, Carly, you're not too old for jeggings." But she would be more dressed up than Andy in such an outfit. She pulled the blouse off the hanger and headed for the stairs as she said goodbye to her friend.

"Maybe I have a skirt that would look good with this...."

A half hour later, she was in danger of being late. She didn't want to arrive too early, but in enough time to mingle and thank Chelsea and Kelly for having her. Half her wardrobe littered her bed, and she'd settled on a pair of faux leather pants to go with the blouse. Her makeup done just-so, and her hair in a crown braid, she finally felt ready to leave the loft.

Lawrence had said she didn't need to bring anything, but she'd run by the bakery and picked up a couple loaves of pumpkin bread anyway. She couldn't show up empty handed.

Nerves assaulted her the entire way out to Three Rivers Ranch. Only a couple of cars sat in Chelsea's driveway, and Andy pulled into the parking lot of Courage Reins. Then she could leave whenever she wanted to.

She gripped the bread like a shield as she walked to the door. She didn't need to knock. Lawrence leaned in the doorway as she ascended the steps.

"Hey." He reached for the bread. "I said you didn't have to bring anything."

"I know," she said. "I wanted to, though."

The Ninth Inning

He didn't move out of the way, and the space to slip by seemed impossibly small for her to navigate.

"You look fantastic." He scanned her from head to toe and back before offering her his arm. "C'mon in."

Inside the house, warmth radiated from every wall, every person. Chelsea stood in the kitchen with Kelly, as well as Heidi Ackerman. The two of them seemed to be getting a lesson from Heidi about something. Another older couple—Kelly's parents—sat on the couch talking with Frank Ackerman.

Lawrence introduced Andy, though Ivory Armstrong had been her third grade teacher.

"So good to see you." Ivory got up from the couch and hugged her. "How's things since your momma passed?"

Heat gathered behind Andy's eyes, but she willed it away. She'd spent too much time perfecting her makeup to cry now. "I'm okay," she said honestly. "More lonely than anything else." At that moment, she remembered how close Lawrence lingered. His eyes hooked hers, a sense of determination darting across his face.

Mrs. Armstrong patted her hand, and a sense of understanding passed between them. Andy smiled at her, then leaned in and hugged her. "Thanks, Mrs. Armstrong."

"I've told you for years. Call me Ivory."

Gratitude welled in the back of her throat. "I just keep trying, and I can't." As she moved away from the living room, she offered up a prayer.

Thank you for getting me out here today. She pressed her eyes closed, the same words bobbing against her vocal cords. She stretched up and said, "Thank you, Lawrence."

It wasn't exactly the same as her prayer, but she spoke it with just as much sincere emotion.

He brushed his lips along her forehead, a whisper of a touch. But it ignited a fire along her skin that trailed down into her belly.

"Andy brought bread," he told the ladies in the kitchen, and Chelsea turned.

"Andy." She embraced Andy, and another sigh radiated through her body. When she'd broke things off with Lawrence, she'd lost several of her friends too. Namely these women out here at Three Rivers. They didn't get to town much, and she didn't come to the ranch very often, so their socializing had dwindled to the picnic after church.

She glanced between Andy and Lawrence. "Which one of you wants to take over making the gravy?"

Andy stepped forward. "If you trust him in the kitchen, we'll be heading to town to find an open Chinese restaurant."

The Ninth Inning

Lawrence laughed and Chelsea joined in. "Well, my mother has great cooking lessons, Lawrence." She nudged him. "And we all know the way to a woman's heart is through a homecooked meal."

Some of the joy flowing through Andy turned to ash, but Lawrence kept his smile hitched in place. "I thought it was the other way around, Miss Chelsea."

"No, sir," she said as Pete came down the stairs with their daughter. "Isn't that right, Lieutenant? Women love men who can cook for them."

He handed her the little girl. "Porter's still asleep. This little miss wants juice." He appraised Lawrence and then Andy. She felt small under the commanding cowboy's gaze, but he softened it with a smile.

"That's how I won over Chelsea. Banned her from the kitchen completely. After that fire—"

"There was no fire!" she yelled from her bent-over position inside the fridge. "Just smoke. *No* fire."

"She used a fire extinguisher."

She rolled her eyes as she poured juice into a sippy cup.

"Anyway," Pete said, chuckling. "Women do like it when you cook for them."

"How about you make the gravy, then?" Kelly stepped next to him and slapped a whisk into his chest.

"That's just fine." He glanced around. "Where's Squire?"

"Waiting for Libby to wake up."

"Carly just texted," Chelsea announced. "They'll be here in about ten minutes."

"Then we'll almost be ready to eat," Chelsea's mom said. "Want me to go get Squire? I can sit at your place until the baby wakes up."

Kelly shook her head. "No, I'll just call him and tell him to wake her up. It's Thanksgiving. We should be together." She moved a few feet out of the kitchen, a phone to her ear.

Andy felt useless loitering in the kitchen, the table already set, with nothing to add to the conversation. She drifted to Lawrence's side, who'd retreated near the steps, out of the way, but still involved.

The hustle and bustle of the house reminded Andy of growing up in their small farmhouse on the edge of town. Or what used to be the edge of town—Three Rivers had grown a bit over the past two decades. She and her two older brothers crammed into two bedrooms and used one bathroom. Mama always had food for whoever needed it, not just her own family, and they hosted someone for dinner almost every night.

A powerful wave of missing rolled over Andy, and Lawrence must've noticed because he slipped his fingers into hers.

"I'm glad you came," he said, low and through lips that barely moved. "You okay?"

The Ninth Inning

A zing shot up her arm at his touch, the gentleness in his voice. "I'm just missin' Mama."

He squeezed her fingers. "Where are your brothers this year?"

"In-laws," she said. And Daddy had passed away a decade ago, leaving only Andy—and her boutique—in Three Rivers.

Lawrence released her hand as Squire entered the house with Finn at his side and a still-sleepy eyed Libby. "Carly and Reese just pulled up."

He left the front door open for them, and Andy got swept away in Carly's hug and Reese's smile. "You came," he said.

"I did." Andy glanced at Lawrence, who looked like he might shoot lasers at Reese. "I'm glad I got invited." And she was. Lawrence had been right. She shouldn't be at home today, alone. So while she wasn't sure where she stood with him yet—if she even *wanted* to stand with him—she knew she'd been led to Three Rivers Ranch for Thanksgiving dinner.

* * *

Lawrence grew more antsy with every passing moment. Andy seemed to blend into the group flawlessly, and why shouldn't she? She'd grown up here, knew these people. He was the outsider, the transplant from the equine therapy center in Amarillo.

Only Pete knew his family owned and operated the Heart Warriors Center—Courage Reins' biggest and closest competition. After all, Lawrence hadn't picked up equine therapy in just a few months. Oh, no. He'd grown up with it in Amarillo.

And he didn't want anyone else to know. He wasn't sure why; just thought they might look at him differently, ask him why he'd chosen Courage Reins over his family's facility. He didn't want to explain that he needed to live his own life, and even if he chose to do the same thing as his father, at least he'd made his own way.

"Time to eat." Chelsea directed people to their spots at the table, and Lawrence sat on one side, sandwiched between Andy and Carly. He exhaled, finally able to relax. He wasn't sure what had kept him so on-edge—besides Andy. But she giggled at something Kelly had said and then took the one-year-old for her while she dashed back into the kitchen for the salt and pepper shakers.

Watching Andy hold the child brought warmth to Lawrence's chest. He'd supported his sister through her pregnancy, held her daughter, loved them both. But the level of admiration flowing through him now, as he saw Andy press a soft kiss to Libby's hair, couldn't be matched.

Kelly returned, took the little girl, and strapped her in a highchair between her and Squire.

"Okay," Chelsea said as she too finished with her children and sat down. "Let's start by going around and saying something we're each thankful for."

Panic squeezed Lawrence's chest. He had a lot to be grateful for—and he was thankful, and he let other people and God know. But what could he say in this group?

The things he could say—*I'm grateful for Three Rivers. I'm grateful for a job. I'm grateful for my friends*—rotated through his mind. He tried to listen to Frank and Heidi, who expressed gratitude for their family.

Reese said, "I'm grateful for my wife."

Carly leaned into him and snuggled close. A flash of jealousy struck Lawrence. He wanted Andy to cuddle with him like that—the way she used to. He sat as straight and still as possible, refusing to look at her.

"My turn," Carly said. "I'm grateful for government grants."

Every eye turned to Lawrence. He cleared his throat. "I'm grateful for old friendships and hope they can become new again." He didn't even know where the words had come from. He hadn't planned to say them. He shifted his attention to Andy, who stared at him like he'd said he was grateful for pneumonia or the grim reaper or something. He slid his hand onto her knee and she jumped.

"Your turn," he said, a smile forming as he felt the tremble in her leg.

She gave a nervous laugh. "I'm grateful for...." Andy glanced around the table, her gaze settling on Lawrence. "An invitation to this meal." She smiled, but he felt the ice in it. She leaned forward and shifted her leg from under his touch, giving him a private glare as Kelly spoke.

Lawrence should've felt frustrated at her rejection. Should've wondered what he should've said besides what he did. Should've done just about anything but push Andy when she clearly wasn't ready.

Instead, he scooted a tiny bit closer to her and leaned forward, almost touching her, in the pretense that he was trying to see and listen to Squire. But honestly, Lawrence had no idea what the man said. Pete went last, and then Chelsea declared it time to eat.

Andy leaned back and bumped into him. "Excuse me." Her voice could've lanced him with icicles.

"No problem." He didn't move away.

"Back up," she hissed through clenched teeth as she spooned creamed corn onto her plate.

Lawrence chuckled, sure he'd made his intentions

The Ninth Inning

for the invitation to dinner clear, and gave her the distance she wanted. What he wanted, he couldn't quite have. He leaned over to Carly. "How can I get Andy alone to talk to her?"

She heard him, but she didn't answer right away, instead contributing to the argument Reese was having with Will Armstrong about the Dallas Cowboys. In fact, she didn't answer him at all through the rest of the meal. It ended, and the group moved into the great room on the opposite side of the stairs. Pete produced a stack of games, and laughter and fun passed the next hour.

"How about a walk before pie?" Carly asked, glancing around. She lingered on Lawrence as she tucked her arm into Reese's. "We'll go slow."

"Good idea," Squire said. "Let the kids run for a bit."

Jackets slid over shoulders and shoes were found for children, and Lawrence waited until everyone had left just to make sure Andy went with them. She positioned herself with Chelsea and Kelly while the men took the kids farther down the road and into the Ackerman's bigger backyard.

Carly and Reese, Heidi and Frank, and Ivory and Will climbed the steps to the Ackerman's deck and sat down.

Lawrence tagged along behind the women, desperation flooding him. How could he talk to Andy now? She wouldn't like him pulling her away, wouldn't want to be seen going off with him alone—though she used to love to sneak away with him for a stolen kiss in the barn.

Another of their little secrets.

Instead of trying to do something he didn't know how to do, he joined Squire and Pete as they threw a football back and forth. Lawrence kept his focus there, and where Andy disappeared to, he didn't know.

Pete tossed the ball to Finn. "So, Lawrence, you gettin' back together with Andy?"

"No." The word came automatically and sounded a tad on the defensive side. He didn't like the look Pete exchanged with Squire.

He expected Pete, ever the observant lieutenant, to press the issue, find out the truth. But he just said, "Oh, okay," and caught the ball Squire threw his way.

Several minutes later, Carly called, "Lawrence! I need you up here."

"Duty calls." He left the game and mounted the steps. "Yeah?"

She pointed across the road, down toward Brynn's new facilities. "She went that way two minutes ago. Alone."

Lawrence could've hugged Carly. Instead he said, "Thanks, Carly," and bolted down the steps.

The Ninth Inning

"Go slow!" Reese called after him, but Lawrence couldn't make his heart go slow, or his legs, or his ideas.

He found Andy around the back of the arena, the barn between her and everyone else on the homestead. She stood facing the open range, her back to him. Her dark hair blew in the winter wind, and she clutched the throat of her jacket closed with tight fingers.

"Mind if I join you?"

She shrugged and he leaned against the fence next to her, looked out in the same direction she was.

"You okay?" he asked.

"Why didn't you ever tell me about your family?"

Her question caused fireworks to explode in Lawrence's brain. He knew the answer, but didn't want to say it out loud.

"I mean, if we're going to make this old friendship new again, I think you should be more forthcoming." She didn't sound mad, or happy, or teasing. Lawrence couldn't figure out how she felt, and unease tripped through his body.

"Also, had I known you had a sister in Amarillo—a sister at all—I might not have assumed you were dating her." Folding her arms, she shifted her weight away from him, her message clear.

Lawrence watched the dead grasses lean in the wind. "I didn't tell you, because I didn't want you to know what a failure I am."

She finally turned and looked at him. "Why would you be a failure for having a family?"

He didn't expect anyone else to understand. "They don't know where I am," he said. "They don't know what I do. If they did...trust me, I'm a disappointment."

Cheryl, five years younger than Lawrence, didn't work with horses. She'd never wanted to, and somehow that was okay. But if Lawrence didn't want the equine therapy organization his parents had dedicated their lives to, suddenly he'd committed the crime of the century.

"My sister, Cheryl, by the way. Her name is Cheryl. Her baby's name is Ruthann. She moved to San Antonio right after she had the baby." He looked at Andy, really let her see whatever she wanted to see. "My parents didn't treat her well."

She reached up like she'd touch his face, but her hand dropped to her side and she tucked it in her jacket pocket. "Do your parents treat you well?"

"They wanted me to take over the family business." Lawrence looked away. "I didn't want to."

"What was the family business?"

"Nothing." He turned and started back toward the homestead. He didn't want to have this conversation. This was why he hadn't told her anything about his family in the six months they'd dated.

"Lawrence." She hurried to catch him, pulled on

his arm to get him to stop from entering the barn. Sparks raced through his body, though her skin hadn't touched his.

"Come on," she said.

"Come on, what, Andy?" He made himself as tall as he could. "You made it real clear you aren't interested in getting back together. I'm not gonna bare my soul now." He yanked open the barn door and went inside, half-hoping she'd follow him, demand he tell her more, confess that she *was* interested in getting back together.

She didn't; the barn door banged closed behind him. He continued past Pete and Chelsea's, across the parking lot where Andy had left her car, and between the silos and the chicken pens.

His cabin sat third in line, and he dang near tore off the door when he entered. He paced the small living room, trying to decide what to do. His temper rarely made an appearance, but if there was one thing that could drive him mad in less than a heartbeat, it was talk of his family.

So what if he'd left his parents and their equine therapy unit?

So what that he hadn't been able to find anything else that he liked nearly as much, even after years of trying?

So what that his pride had prevented him from

ever going home again? Ever apologizing? Ever making things right?

His parents didn't know that he'd made practically nothing of his life.

No one knew. No one needed to know, especially not the beautiful, successful Andrea Larsen.

Chapter Four

"Are you sure about this?" Andy looked at the pie plate as vipers bit their way through her system. "He was really mad."

She'd never seen Lawrence get mad, ever. In their six months together, he'd been calm and collected and soft-spoken and soothing. He'd made her feel special by coming to her store and helping her with inventory, or just watching her hang clothes after she'd flipped the sign to closed.

She'd come out to the ranch and watch his therapy lessons, and they'd walk through the fields, and he'd taught her about horses. True, he'd never said anything about his family, and while Andy had wondered at the time, she hadn't found it odd. He was mysterious, and handsome, and she'd assumed he'd tell her when he was ready.

"Of course I'm sure." Carly's voice pulled Andy from her memories. "Every man loves pie, and this is chocolate cookie pie." She straightened Andy's blouse. "Right, girls?"

Kelly nodded, and Chelsea stepped forward. "I brought Pete a pie once. It seemed to work, because he came to dinner the next day."

Andy didn't want Lawrence to come to dinner with her. Or maybe she did. Everything jumbled inside her, and she didn't know what she wanted.

"So you march over there," Kelly said.

"And you knock nicely," Chelsea added. "No banging."

"When he answers, you give him the pie, and say you missed him at the house and thought he might want this." Carly smiled. "Then you say that you could barely eat because you can't stand the thought of him upset, and ask him if he'd like to share it with you." She brandished two forks. "Ask him to walk out on the range. He likes that."

"And you won't have to go in his cabin," Kelly added. "He might not want you in there if he's…a tiny bit upset."

"He's mad," Andy said, eyeing the forks like they'd stab her on the way to Lawrence's cabin.

"Don't beg him to go with you," Chelsea said. "If

The Ninth Inning

he doesn't want to come, take both forks and head out on the range alone. That'll get him to come."

"Why will that get him to come?" Andy wondered how these women knew so much about how to win over a man.

"Because, silly, he won't want you out on the range alone." Chelsea smiled and squeezed Andy's shoulder. "And there's a storm comin' in. He definitely won't let you wander off on your own."

"Okay, ready?" Kelly took a deep breath, and Andy mimicked her.

"Ready as I'll ever be." She took the forks from Carly and headed outside. The sky had turned a threatening shade of navy blue, and by the time she knocked—nicely—on Lawrence's door, the air held the promise of rain.

Lawrence whipped the door open and stared at her.

"Hey," she started. "I brought you some pie, since you missed dessert." She held the plate, which held half of a chocolate cookie pie, toward him with one hand. She'd forgotten what to say next, but the presence of the silverware in her other hand reminded her.

"I didn't get to eat any either," she said. "I was too worried about you. Want to share?"

His blue eyes sparked lightning in her direction. Sometime during lunch she'd decided to give

Lawrence another chance. Give *them* another chance. Or maybe she'd been stewing over a second chance with him since he'd lured her out to the ranch and invited her to Thanksgiving dinner. She wasn't sure.

When he didn't move, or invite her in, or speak at all, she said, "Well, okay. I'm going to take a walk and find a place to eat my pie." She adjusted the plastic wrap on the plate, turned and moved down his steps, pivoted to go between the cabins and onto the range. Her throat tightened with fear. Everything looked exactly the same out here. What if she really got lost?

"Where you goin'?" he called after her.

"Pie." She lifted the forks and kept walking. The wind nearly stole the dessert from her, but she plowed on. She spied a tree in the distance, and she thought she could make it there and back safely enough.

"Andy, this is insane." Lawrence ran up beside her. "It's going to rain any second."

She looked at him and couldn't look away. "Well, I can't go back to Chelsea's now. It'll be too embarrassing."

"What do you mean?"

"I mean I had to tell them about you stomping off and leaving me, and I can't do that again."

"Like how you rejected me at dinner?"

"I wasn't ready for what you said." She stopped, her anger overshadowing her embarrassment and fear.

"And you shouldn't have touched me like that. It really put me on the spot."

Thunder broke the sky; lightning flashed above them.

He stared at her, and she couldn't figure out how to feel. Should she just tell him she missed him, the way he had? Confess that every time she'd considered deleting his number from her phone, she got physically ill? Confide in him and say she imagined kissing him every time she opened the storeroom?

"You are a maddening woman." He strode forward again, breaking the spell between them before Andy could decide what to do.

"You're just as frustrating," she said as she rushed to catch him. But his long legs made her have to take three steps for every two of his.

"I have one sister. That's all. We get along great. My parents are another story."

Andy didn't know what to add to the conversation; she just wanted him to keep talking.

"They run the Heart Warriors center in Amarillo. I didn't want to do that. I left when I was eighteen. Haven't been back in a decade." His short sentences were punctuated by his long strides. "I thought I didn't want to work with horses and patients. I thought I wanted something else. When Courage Reins opened...well, I got a job here, and I realized I loved it.

What I didn't love was being told what I had to do with my life."

He stopped suddenly and faced her. "I should go home. I should take over the program for my parents. But I don't want to. I don't want Reese's job, or Pete's job. I don't want the responsibility. I just want to work with the horses and the patients. That's enough for me. It won't be enough for my dad."

"That doesn't make you a failure."

He gave a short, barking laugh. "No, it doesn't. You're right. What makes me a failure is everything else I tried until I figured out I'm just a horseman." He stomped off again, leaving Andy to wonder what was so wrong with being a horseman.

LAWRENCE COULDN'T BELIEVE he'd told Andy everything—well, maybe not everything. But he did trust her, and she did deserve the truth. He hated that he'd gotten angry when she'd asked about his family. She'd given him an hour to cool off, and if anything, seeing her on his doorstep with pie had kicked his desire for her into a new gear.

She caught up to him just as the first raindrops fell. He paused, judging the distance to the tree. Too far. He turned and looked back at the row of cabins.

The Ninth Inning

"We're going to get soaked." He looked down at her. She wore her jacket and those sexy tight pants. No hat. No gloves. At least the pie was covered with plastic wrap.

"I don't care." She put the pie on the ground and stepped into his arms.

He welcomed her into his embrace, surprised at this turn of events but not complaining. "You don't?"

The sky opened and water poured out. They were both soaked through in seconds. She tilted her head up, taking partial refuge under the brim of his cowboy hat. "I do want some of that pie. But I guess it can wait."

"Hmm." He wasn't sure why it needed to wait, but he couldn't look away from Andy, from the raindrops on her eyelashes, from the pinkness of her lips. She licked them, and he reacted by pressing his mouth to hers.

She melted into him, threaded her fingers through his hair, and kissed him back.

Hours could've passed and Lawrence wouldn't have known. Kissing Andy had always possessed a bit of magic, and this time felt downright divine. With the rain pounding down around them, he kissed her and kissed her, hoping this was only the beginning of what they could have together.

When he detected a wobble in her chin, he pulled back. "Cold?"

"Just a little." She brushed her lips along his. "We should go back before we freeze, though."

He bent to retrieve the pie, tucked her hand in his, and ran toward his cabin. She came with him, which caused joy to punctuate the perfect kiss.

Once under the safety of his porch, he looked her up and down. "Uh, you're going to need dry clothes."

"I'll wear something of yours while you run the dryer."

"Uh, Andy? My stuff is way too big for you." He opened the front door and ushered her inside the cabin. "Maybe you can borrow something of Juliette's." He didn't want her asking Kelly or Chelsea. He might never get her back if she went over to one of their houses to borrow clothes.

"Aren't they in Montana?"

"I have a key to Garth's place." Lawrence plucked it from the drawer in his kitchen. "Stay here. I'll be right back." He hurried out the door and down the path. Surely she'd wait, right? She wouldn't kiss him the way she had and then disappear into the night.

He dashed into Garth's cabin and hurried into the bedroom. He grabbed the first thing of Juliette's he saw in the closet—a sundress—and hightailed it out of there. When he got back to his cabin, Andy had the inklings of a fire going in the hearth.

The Ninth Inning

"Grabbed the first thing I saw," he said. "I felt weird doing that."

She took the dress. "This is fine. I'm not good at making a fire. I'll change, and you finish that?"

She disappeared into the bathroom, and Lawrence stood staring at the closed door. When he'd invited her to dinner, he didn't think he'd end up kissing her. Never in his wildest—okay, maybe in his *wildest* dreams, he thought she might let him.

She came out of the bathroom holding her wet things, the pink sundress complementing her dark hair and skin. He sucked in a breath and focused on what he should be doing. He took her clothes and ducked into his bedroom to change and start the dryer.

With that all done, he got the fire going properly, and pulled two blankets from the front closet. He gave one to Andy, who wrapped herself in it before settling on his couch. "Got any movies?" She yawned. "All that turkey is catching up to me."

"No napping until after pie." He put his blanket on the other end of the couch, nudged up the heat, and moved into the kitchen to collect the pie. "Movies are in the cabinet next to the hearth."

He grabbed silverware and returned to the living room. "Can I sit here?" He indicated the spot right next to where she'd been sitting. "Then we can share the pie."

"Yeah." She held up a case. "This one okay?"

He didn't care what they watched. Excitement to simply be with her made his nerve endings dance. "Yeah, fine."

She slid in the disc, handed him the remotes, and took her place on the couch. He passed her a fork, adjusted the volume, and started the movie. They ate in silence, Lawrence's mind spinning through where this could go next.

He'd never told anyone about his family, and it felt good to get the weight off his tongue. Andy hadn't asked him about what he'd done in the past eight years before landing at Courage Reins, nor had she seemed to judge him for leaving his family just to become what he'd already been.

He felt insignificant next to her, and a pinch started behind his heart. Could she really want someone like him? The constant struggle, the familiar battle, raged as strongly now as it had the first time they'd been together.

"You done?" she asked as she scooped up another bite. "You've stopped eating."

"Just thinking," he said.

"About what?" She abandoned the movie in favor of him. "Kissin' me again?" Her playful tone and twinkling eyes sent heat through his core.

"*Now* that's what I'm thinking about." He leaned

over and tasted her whipped cream lips.

"Mmm, tasty." Her whispered words caused a shiver to shake his spine.

He touched his lips to hers again. "I was thinking about why you want to be with me."

She pulled back a couple of inches to look into his eyes. She searched and searched, and he didn't know if she found what she wanted or not. "Why wouldn't I want to be with you?"

"Why did it take me ordering something from your boutique to get you to apologize?"

"Same reason you haven't gone home in ten years."

Pride. He understood that. Couldn't blame her for it, though they probably should both get over being too proud to apologize to those they loved. Not that she loved him. Lawrence cut off his thoughts before they could derail.

"And you really want to be with a horseman? Someone like you...." He trailed off, unsure and unwilling to let her see how weak he felt, how inadequate. He kissed her again, grateful when she returned the gesture.

Grateful he didn't have to explain anything else.

Grateful she stayed in his arms through the rest of the movie, long after her clothes had dried.

Grateful God had brought her back to him, at least for one day, though Lawrence prayed for a lot longer.

Chapter Five

Andy puzzled through Lawrence's words as she bustled around the shop, the two other ladies she'd hired just for Black Friday as busy as she was. No matter how often she circled the store, she found more tops that needed to be refolded, additional tissue paper that had fallen from inside sweaters, hangers that needed to be straightened.

She didn't complain, instead pressing her eyes closed for a brief moment of gratitude with every sale. The holiday season kept Andy afloat during the slower winter months. Still, her mind wandered to Lawrence as she selected sizes and styles and colors.

The bitterness and longing in his tone when he mentioned he was just a horseman. The way he pondered why she wanted to be with him. She obviously wasn't the only one who had her eye on

Lawrence, whether he knew it or not. But she couldn't believe he missed the constantly vulturistic women at the church picnics.

She'd just gotten him out of her mind when her phone blared, bringing him right back in. Because the ringtone belonged to him. Silencing it, she flashed an apologetic smile to the woman preparing to purchase two pairs of slacks and a trio of holiday sweaters. She shoved the phone in a drawer behind the cash register, determined to focus on her boutique until she could afford to donate some brain cells to Lawrence.

Her holiday hours extended well past normal, and by the time she locked the door, her feet felt like she'd walked across live coals. She heaved herself upstairs before she realized she'd left her phone in that blasted drawer downstairs.

Too tired to go retrieve it, she fell into an Epsom salt bath, knowing she had to redo what she'd done today all over again tomorrow. Though Sundays had been a source of loneliness for her, she suddenly couldn't wait until she could have her day of rest.

Sunday came, as Sundays always did, and Andy took her usual seat near the back of the chapel. She'd almost skipped church today—surely God would've given her a pass because of the exhausting nature of the last forty-eight hours.

If she were being honest with herself—something

she'd been trying to do more recently—she hoped to see Lawrence at church. She'd even sat down from the end of the pew so he could slide in next to her whenever he happened to arrive. She'd even come early so he'd see her.

Her patience was rewarded when a warm arm settled across her shoulders, and the leather and horse scent met her nose, and the handsomeness of Lawrence's face filled her vision. "This seat taken?"

"It is now." She leaned into him, satisfied when he cupped her shoulder and pulled her a bit closer.

A group of women slid onto the bench next to Andy right when the service started, but she didn't pay much attention to them. They whispered through the first fifteen minutes, and it wasn't until one of them spoke a little too loudly that she turned toward them.

But she heard the word "boutique," and she owned the only boutique in town. Suddenly, her ears went into owl-mode, flicking and zeroing in on the conversation. She couldn't hear much, because the choir got up and began singing.

But those women were definitely talking about her. Her and Lawrence.

Andy straightened under his arm and lifted her chin. If they wanted to gossip, she'd let them. In fact, maybe she should give them something to talk about.

Wicked thoughts ran through her mind, but she

didn't act on any of them. She already had enough on her plate this holiday season; she didn't need to add more to it.

The service ended, and she stood.

"You in a hurry?" Lawrence asked, peering up at her from under his cowboy hat.

"Well, no."

"Did you make anything for lunch?"

She hadn't even thought about lunch. Andy usually grabbed something from the fridge or called in take-out during the busy season. At the moment, she couldn't remember what, if anything, her fridge held.

"What did you make?" she asked to save herself from admitting anything.

"I'm sure you don't want food poisoning going into the busiest time of the year." He grinned and added a chuckle to his statement.

"I probably have a frozen pizza."

"I was just gonna say I'm really craving a frozen pizza." He leaned back into the bench and grinned.

A flush rose to her face. "Are you inviting yourself to my place for lunch?" She wondered if he'd stay for dinner too. The man was hopeless when it came to cooking.

He finally stood. Most of the other churchgoers had already left the chapel, including the gossipers. "I haven't been to your place for a while," he said. "Seems like a good time to check it out."

Stepping into the aisle, he offered Andy his hand. She slipped her fingers into his, a thrill trailing down her back. The storeroom dominated her thoughts as he followed her to the boutique, as they parked in the narrow driveway behind the building, as he captured her hand again and they moved up the back steps.

The storeroom sat just inside the door, but Andy refused to look at it. She continued into the shop and swept her hand toward the area. "It's kind of a mess right now," she said. "I'll come clean it up later." She sighed just thinking about it. But she couldn't open on Monday morning without clean floors and crisp folds in the clothes. She'd spend an hour this evening straightening and creasing, and everything would be set for the next day.

"It's so festive." Lawrence admired the set of Christmas trees Andy had set up late on Thanksgiving night, after one of the most perfect evenings she'd ever spent with a man. She'd also trailed lights along the check-out counter, around the mirrors on the west wall and lining the windows on the east.

A pine-scented candle warmer sat next to the front door, and another next to the till. Her mannequins wore the most festive and spirited holiday items, and if she flicked on the stereo system,

Christmas music would complete the picture-perfect atmosphere.

Lawrence paced a few steps away, fingered a red bow skirt on a mannequin and twisted back to her. "I didn't see the shop at Christmas last year. It's fantastic." He beamed at her, and something in Andy's gut jumped.

He adored her. She could see it, right there on his face. Anyone would be able to see it. Suddenly self-conscious, she turned away, unsure if she deserved such adoration. He hadn't seen the shop last Christmas because she'd freaked out before she'd gotten the facts and broken things off with him.

"Let's see about that pizza." She headed upstairs, all fantasies about the storeroom shelved for now.

THE FOLLOWING SUNDAY, Andy arrived last to church, grateful Lawrence had saved a sliver of space for her on a pew near the back. Seemed like more and more people were coming out for services, probably because of the approaching Christmas season.

She enjoyed Pastor Scott's sermon, which focused on living more like the Savior. Andy wanted to do that, wanted to be as forgiving and loving as the Lord. She tried to be kind to those she came in contact with, but they usually were potential customers. She thought of the twittering women who'd sat next to her last week. Would she be as kind to them after knowing they'd been speaking about her?

Frustration sparked at the truth flowing through her mind. She probably wouldn't be. And it had taken a ruse to get her to apologize to Lawrence.

A frown buckled her eyebrows. *Why did it take me a year to apologize?* she wondered.

The service ended, leaving a multitude of questions in Andy's mind, and she stood with Lawrence.

Pete stepped up to them. "Lawrence, I need you for a second." He nodded toward someone exiting the chapel. "That's Bobby Haskins."

Lawrence obviously knew who Bobby Haskins was, and why he was important, because he turned and said, "Give me a minute, okay, Andy?" He didn't wait for her to answer before he moved down the aisle with Pete and Reese.

Andy assumed their business with Bobby had something to do with Courage Reins, and she moved a little further into the chapel to help Chelsea clean up after her kids. By the time they toddled down the aisle with the littles, Andy assumed Lawrence would be finished with his business.

Nobody waited in the lobby, but Pete came through the door and swept Julie onto his shoulders.

The Ninth Inning

"You good?" he asked Chelsea, and they stepped out of the church.

Andy followed in their wake, freezing as soon as she moved outside. The door bumped her, pushing her forward. She stumbled as her brain tried to make sense of the scene before her.

Lawrence stood several feet away, far enough to keep his words from Andy. But his mouth moved, and he grinned at the group of women who'd gathered around him. The group of single women.

She and Lawrence hadn't made lunch plans, but Andy had assumed. Assumed he'd be coming over for something to eat—she'd even run to the grocery store last night to have a variety of frozen meals on hand. He hadn't seemed to mind the pizza from last week, though it bore the marks of some freezer burn and she didn't have any extra cheese to add to the top.

He'd eaten a lot of it, stayed for a movie, kissed her until her legs couldn't hold her weight. She'd been hoping for a repeat today, but now, the sight of all those women blurred her fantasies.

She blinked and shook her head. She'd seen Lawrence talking to, laughing with, and helping another woman once. She'd jumped to the wrong conclusion that his sister was his date, just because he paid for dinner. Was she destined to repeat that same mistake now?

Jealousy roared through her, making her stomach turn and her throat burn. The real question became: Did she trust Lawrence or not?

You have to trust him, she told herself as she made her way down the steps on wobbling heels. *Help me trust him.*

She feared, though, that all the self-talk and all the prayer in the world couldn't make her do something she didn't know how to do.

Lawrence chuckled at Natalie, the woman from the Three Rivers women's association. She wanted him to bring some of the horses from Courage Reins to a family carnival the group was planning for the spring.

He'd told her he didn't have the authority to say yes or no, but that he'd ask Pete. He liked Natalie and played golf with her brother from time to time. He wanted to support the women, and he made easy conversation with them while he waited for Andy to come out.

Movement caught his attention, and he found her coming toward them, her face a quivering mask of emotion. He couldn't decipher how she felt as she neared and smoothed over her true feelings with a smile.

The Ninth Inning

"Ladies, do you know Andy Larsen?" He drew her into his side, clearly claiming her as his. Every woman there catalogued the movement, Lawrence made sure of it. "Andy, these ladies are from the Three Rivers women's association." He named them all, pleased at his own memory.

"Well, let me know, Lawrence," Natalie said. The ladies made themselves scarce after that, leaving Lawrence to practically drag Andy to her car.

"You okay?" he asked as they neared. "You don't look so good."

"I don't feel so good," she said. "I hope you weren't planning to come for lunch."

"Of course I was." He leaned against her car, noticing the glassiness in her eyes. "What's wrong?"

She shook her head and caught the tear as it fell from her eye. "Nothing. I just need to lie down. I feel sick."

Lawrence had the sick feeling he'd done something wrong. But he didn't know what. "I'll follow you home. Make sure you're okay."

"No." She reached for the door handle. "I'll make it."

"I can heat you up some of that canned soup you have in your cupboard."

She managed a slight glare. "How do you know I have canned soup in my cupboard?"

He gave her a slow grin. "Saw it last week." Stepping away from the car, Lawrence pulled out his keys. "I'll follow you home."

She might have argued, but Lawrence didn't quite hear it as he strode toward his truck. She could lock him out if he didn't arrive close to the same time as her. Thankfully, Andy wasn't the fastest driver in the world, and he pulled in right after her. She let him in the shop, but he sensed something was still off.

The door had barely closed when he asked, "Are you going to tell me what I did wrong?"

"Nothing," she said, bending to remove her heels. "You didn't do anything wrong."

He moved closer and took her into his arms. She came willingly, a good sign. "Then why were you cryin' at the church?"

Embarrassment stole across her expression. "I don't want to tell you." She squirmed to get out of his grip, and he let her go. "It's just something I need to work on," she said. "It honestly has nothing to do with you." She moved toward the stairs that led to her loft.

"Honestly?" he asked as he followed.

"Cross my heart," she tossed over her shoulder. At the top of the stairs, she pushed into her living space, which consisted of the entire second floor of the building. Everything Andy touched had an air of sophistication about it, and the sitting room at the entrance of her loft was no exception. Lawrence barely knew how to exist in such a refined space, and he wondered what she thought of his simple, country cowboy cabin.

He also knew she owned this building, had inherited it from her daddy when he'd died. Andy had no debts, and a heap of success. Lawrence felt seven shades of inadequate standing in her loft.

Why now, he wasn't sure. Last Sunday, he'd been okay. Fine, he'd shaken off the feelings of self-loathing and charmed his way into staying for lunch, a movie, and a passionate embrace that had ended too soon for his liking.

"You comin'?" she called from farther inside the loft. "I'm not making these pot pies by myself."

He gave himself a mental and physical shake, removed his jacket and hung it on the antique iron coat rack, as if he could remove his shortcomings as easily, and followed her into the gourmet kitchen.

If she could pretend like she was fine, so could he.

Chapter Six

"You like that Natalie Cooper?" Andy couldn't help herself. She'd been stewing over the other women for the last hour since seeing Lawrence talking to her. While she drove home, while he asked her if she was okay, while the turkey pot pies browned and bubbled and baked.

He glanced up as if a gunshot had sounded. "What? Definitely not." He stuffed a forkful of green beans—canned and heated in the microwave—into his mouth. His face reddened as he chewed and swallowed. "I mean, I like her just fine. She's nice. But I'm not...you know. I don't *like* her."

Andy pushed her food around inside the pie shell. "What did she want?"

Lawrence stared at her for several moments past

comfortable. Andy finally lifted her eyes to his. "What?"

"You think I was—" He set his fork down, his food forgotten. "Well, what exactly did you think, Andy?"

She didn't like the resentment in his tone, the piercing slice of his gaze. Though he had every right to be upset, Andy wished he wasn't. Wished she hadn't said anything. Wished she didn't automatically assume the worst about him.

"Nothing," she tried, but Lawrence scoffed.

"You think I want to be with one of those women more than you." He pushed away from the table and stood. "You think eventually I'll cheat on you with one of them. Is that it?"

Helplessness made her stomach quake, her bottom lip tremble. "You're awfully handsome," she said. "And hardworking, and honest, and—"

"Are you tryin' to pay me a compliment or tell me you don't trust me?" He sat heavily in the chair again, his voice a mere ghost of itself, but his eyes as penetrating as ever.

Both, Andy thought, but kept the word contained in her mind. Thankfully.

Emboldened by her decision to start being more truthful with him—and herself—she looked at him. She put both her hands on one of his, wishing she could erase the anguished expression from his face.

"I—I want to be with you." The admission rang with truth, though it wasn't the one she needed to say.

"But you don't trust me." He kept his hand under hers in a fist, unwilling or unable to soften it and let her hold his hand.

She dropped her eyes to the table. The small table he could barely fold himself under without crowding her. The small table where she wanted to eat breakfast with him. And lunch. And dinner. The strength of her thoughts surprised her, and she didn't know how to make them line up with the jealousy and bitterness she'd felt at the church.

"All right." He slid his hand out from under hers. "I'm gonna head home."

"No," she said. "You don't need to go."

"I think I do, Andy." He stood, and she couldn't argue with the quiet strength in his voice. Couldn't get up and follow him through the living room. Couldn't make her voice say, "Don't go. Stay and let's talk about this."

The door closed and she heard his cowboy boots clomp down her stairs. The old building shuddered as he left the shop, and Andy dropped her head into her hands. Why had she said anything? Or at least phrased it like, "Hey, what did Natalie Cooper want?" instead of making it an accusation.

The Ninth Inning

Eyes brimming with tears, she set about cleaning up the remains of their lunch. She'd barely eaten two bites, and yet her stomach waged war against her. She'd felt like this for the whole holiday season last year. She didn't think she could survive another one. To keep her hands as busy as her mind, she moved from the eat-in kitchen into the living room and vacuumed the rugs she'd special-ordered from New York. She dusted the shelves holding the pictures of her and Mama. Tears trickled down her face while she completed the long overdue chore.

But this time, they didn't belong to Mama.

This time, they trailed tracks down her cheeks for Lawrence.

She flung down the duster and rushed across the room and into the entryway. A sob choked her as she yanked open the door and flew down the stairs. Outside, her chest heaved. Lawrence's truck was long gone. Of course it was. She'd been cleaning for a good twenty minutes.

She hated this feeling. This feeling of waiting for something to happen so she could stop feeling so anxious. Of constantly searching for him in crowds so she could either worry when he wasn't there or relax when he was.

Andy didn't know what to do, short of getting in her sedan and driving out to the ranch. But too many eyes and ears existed out there. Too much of an audience for her private business.

She returned to her loft and snatched her phone from the kitchen counter. Her fingers fumbled over the screen as she brought up Lawrence and pressed call.

It rang once. Twice. Three times. Her heart stalled its beat. He had to answer. Four rings. Why wasn't he answering?

His voicemail picked up, a sore disappointment to the real timbre of his voice. She hung up, defeated. Familiar anxiety and worry and absolute tension gnawed at her until she shook with the effort it took not to collapse on the couch and cry.

Her phone buzzed before it rang, and she startled. Her hopes soared when she saw Lawrence's face.

"Lawrence," she breathed into the line.

"You called?"

"Please come back," she blurted. "You can't be far. Just...please come back." She glanced into the kitchen, though she'd cleaned up his lunch. "You didn't even finish eating."

"That's what you're worried about?" He didn't sound like he was driving. Maybe he'd pulled over to call her. "That I didn't get enough to eat?"

"That's what I always worry about." A nervous giggle escaped her mouth. "I know you can't cook, and yes. I worry about what you eat everyday. I'm scared

The Ninth Inning

you'll get tired of me really fast." The floodgate on her insecurities and fears dropped. "And I'm absolutely terrified that I'll never figure out how to trust you."

She took a deep breath, the weight of her words out in the open, where he could possibly help shoulder them.

"Well," he started. "I get along just fine in the food department. You realize I live next door to Juliette, right? And Chelsea and Kelly aren't bad, either." Something changed on his end of the line, because his voice sounded farther away when he said, "I don't think I'll ever get tired of you, but we can talk about why you'd think so. If you want."

A door closed; her building trembled. "And you do need to figure out how to trust me, Andy. I can't really help you in that department."

A knock sounded on her door, and she spun and crossed the distance to it in the time it took to breathe. She opened the door and lowered the phone when she found Lawrence on the other side.

"But I'll try," he said, stepping into her entryway and sweeping her into an embrace that felt like home.

* * *

Nervous energy punctuated every breath Andy took while she waited for the last customer of the day to make her selections. Lawrence had been waiting upstairs in her loft for twenty minutes. He said he didn't mind, and he probably genuinely didn't.

"I think I like this one." Sandy twisted to look at the back of the jacket.

"It looks fabulous," Andy said, smoothing her fingertips across Sandy's shoulders. "Going somewhere special for Christmas this year?"

Sandy made a face. "Do I ever?"

Andy forced a laugh. "Christmas in Three Rivers isn't the worst."

"I know." Sandy sighed. "I'm just...done here, you know?" She looked at Andy with such honesty, her heartstrings sang.

"You bought the pancake house, didn't you?" Andy asked. "You can't be done here now."

Sandy shrugged out of the jacket and handed it to Andy. "I'll take this and those jeans. And that reindeer sweater. My mother will love that." She flashed a grin at Andy. "And no, I know. I'm not done bein' in Three Rivers." She turned and headed back into the dressing room for her own jacket. "Just done with the men here."

Andy understood that more keenly than she'd like to admit. Once she'd ended things with Lawrence, the men she'd dated had been dull, brash, or just plain annoying. She rang up Sandy's purchases and had

The Ninth Inning

them wrapped when the woman came out of the dressing room.

"Saw Lawrence's truck outside," she said as she added her signature to the receipt. "Am I keeping you from something?"

Andy took the slip of paper and tucked it in the till. She gave Sandy a warm smile. "Not at all. We're just goin' to dinner in a bit."

Sandy took the bag with her new clothes, her own unassuming grin in place. "He's a nice guy."

"Yeah," Andy agreed, beyond relieved when a rush of jealousy didn't threaten to unseat her. "He is."

"Well, Merry Christmas." Sandy headed for the door, and Andy went with her. Once she'd given the proper holiday salutation, she locked the door and flipped the sign to closed. She should stay and clean up for the Saturday crowd. After all, only three weekends left to shop for Christmas.

But she could get up early. Right now, she wanted to see Lawrence, smell Lawrence, kiss Lawrence.

* * *

"Busy week?" Lawrence traced lazy circles on her upper arm as he cradled Andy in his embrace. It had been five long days without her, and now that he had her in his arms, he didn't want to let her go.

"Not bad, actually," she said, snuggling closer. "Thanks for dinner."

"Mm." He'd taken her out to dinner after asking her what she wanted. She'd said, "All the bread and pasta I can get."

Since they'd gotten a later start on dinner, they'd missed the movie he'd been planning to take her to see. So now, they laid on her couch, a movie on but Lawrence wasn't really watching it. He wondered if Andy was.

After last Sunday's situation, he'd been thinking about how he could convince Andy he was trustworthy. He'd spoken true—he couldn't really help her with that. She either believed he wanted to be with her and no one else, or she didn't.

But he had thought he could tell her everything. Be one-hundred-percent honest about his life, lay open his soul, and see if she still wanted him.

The idea had kept him awake at night, and everyone from Juliette to Pete to his patients at Courage Reins had noticed.

Taking a deep breath, he reached for the remote. "You watchin' this?"

"Not really." She sat up and tossed him a guilty grin.

He switched off the TV and ran his hands over his face. "I want to talk to you about something."

The Ninth Inning

"Okay." She held perfectly still, her expression unreadable.

"Remember I said I left home when I was eighteen?"

"Yes."

"I tried to start a business that failed. Cost my folks a lot of money. That's one reason I can't seem to go home and face them." Familiar guilt coated Lawrence's throat, but he swallowed it away. "Don't have much of a head for business."

She blinked at him. "All right."

"Don't you see?" He leaned forward. "You're like, this successful businesswoman, and I couldn't even hack it in the feed industry for more than a year."

Andy sat there, an utterly perplexed look on her face. "I don't get what that has to do with anything."

"I have a lot of debt, that's what." He exhaled sharply. "Maybe this was a bad idea." he studied the swirling pattern in her rug. "I just want to—I think we —" Why couldn't he get his tongue to cooperate with his brain?

"I guess I just wanted you to know." He didn't add that if they were married, his debt would become her problem too. He didn't want to scare Andy away with declarations and proposals too soon. And by the deer-in-the-headlights expression she now wore, he would if he said much more.

"How much debt?" she asked.

"Thousands," he said darkly. "Doesn't help that my ex-wife—" He sucked in the rest of the sentence, his body recoiling from the word—just like Andy's was.

"Ex-wife?" she choked out. She got up and moved into the kitchen, where she filled a glass with water from the tap and gulped it. She leaned against the countertop a good twenty feet from him. "Tell me about her."

Dread filled Lawrence from top to bottom. His legs felt like cement, his heart like dynamite. "I told you I'd done a lot of stupid things. That was one of them."

"Getting married is stupid?"

"Most of the time, no. In my case, it was. Jenn—well, we were only married for two weeks before I had it annulled. But that was enough time to do a lifetime of financial damage."

"Annulled?"

Lawrence didn't like the pitch of Andy's voice.

"Jenn wasn't legally divorced when we got married," he said, practically to himself. "She said it had gone through, but well, it hadn't." Luckily for him. "The charges she put on my credit card during our 'marriage' have been ordered to be paid back. But I'm still waiting for the first check."

Andy folded her arms. "How long ago was this?"

"Five years. I bounced around Texas and Oklahoma for a while until I settled at Three Rivers." Contentment ballooned in Lawrence's chest. "I'm finally getting things together. But I still have some hurdles to overcome. And if you and I—" He cleared his throat, unwilling to say more.

"That's why you were worried about me liking you," she said, some of the stoniness on her face melting away. "Of you just being a horseman."

Lawrence nodded, his voice too knotted to work.

"Well, don't worry about that," she said.

A scoff burst from his mouth. "Right. I'll put that at the top of my to-do list. Don't worry about what the gorgeous, successful, has-it-all-together Andy Larsen thinks of me." He made a slashing motion with his hand. "Check." He shook his head, his tone harsher than he intended. But come on. Did she think it was just that easy to do?

She took a calculated step toward him. "You think I'm gorgeous."

"Uh, yeah."

"Successful?"

"Every woman I see is wearing something that came from this shop."

She invaded his personal space, practically forcing him to meet her eye. "I do not have it all together. Most days I'm hanging on by a thread."

He wanted to argue. Wanted her to take his

concerns more seriously. Wanted to ask if his confessions had helped her to trust him more.

Instead, he leaned down and kissed her, relieved and reassured when she kissed him back.

* * *

Lawrence boosted himself onto the bottom rung of the fence surrounding the indoor arena. "Make 'im go right."

Sariah Swanson, the teen riding Chocolate, nodded, her mouth in a grim line. Sariah came from a town about thirty minutes east of Three Rivers, the victim of a severe fire that left seventy percent of her body covered in scars. Working with the horses gave her a confidence and strength she hadn't possessed six months ago when she'd started.

Lawrence watched her bring Chocolate around again, this time muttering at him and pulling harder on the reins. He obeyed at the last moment, stubborn horse that he was. Or maybe he just wanted Sariah to work for her successes.

She beamed at Lawrence, who gave her a thumbs up and a grin.

"Lawrence?"

He glanced toward Reese, barely taking his eyes from Sariah. "Yeah?"

The Ninth Inning

"There's someone here to see you."

"I'm with—"

"Pete said I should take over."

A pit formed in Lawrence's gut. "Who is it?"

Reese shook his head. "Just go see."

"It's not my mother, is it?" Lawrence couldn't get his feet to move toward the offices of Courage Reins.

"No." Reese didn't take his eyes from Sariah. "She's younger than that."

"My sister?" Urgency flowed through Lawrence now. He'd told her to call him if she needed anything. His phone hadn't rung in months, since he'd helped her move to San Antonio with her baby girl.

Reese shrugged, but the tight set of his mouth suggested Lawrence wouldn't like whoever he met. Besides Cheryl, he couldn't think of a single person who would come looking for him at Three Rivers Ranch.

The walk to the lobby seemed to stretch for miles and he paused at the corner. A woman stood near the front wall of windows, her back to him. She had dark hair and wore jeans and a leather jacket.

Nothing remarkable about her. Maybe she was a new patient.

"Ma'am?" He moved forward. "You asked to see me?"

The woman turned, and still Lawrence found

nothing familiar in her face. She had dark eyes to match her hair, and when she smiled, it was a bit crooked like his.

"Are you Lawrence Collins?"

"Yes." Snakes writhed through his veins. "What can I do for you?"

"I'm Gina Collins." She grinned at him, her eyes watering now. "I'm your half-sister."

Chapter Seven

Andy had barely closed the store after an exhausting Monday—a Monday! Usually one of her quieter days—when her phone sang from inside the drawer. It was Sandy.

"Hey," Andy said. "What's up, Sandy?"

"Okay, I don't normally do this, but I think you better get over to the pancake house."

Andy punched in the code to open the till, none of her nightly chores complete because of the flurry of sales she'd had in the last half hour. "Why?"

"Lawrence just came in."

"Okay." Andy didn't see why this mattered, though an undercurrent of urgency rode in Sandy's tone, something Andy hadn't heard before.

"He's with another woman."

Andy's blood turned to ice. She took a second to

force herself to be rational, to trust Lawrence. "Does she have short hair? Sort of chopped like it was an accident?"

"No—"

"Because that's his sister," Andy practically yelled over Sandy.

"This woman has dark hair. Curled." Sandy's voice dropped to a whisper on the last word. "It's not my business, and like I said, I don't normally do this. But I know y'all were dating last year and then weren't, and now are again, and…I don't want you to get hurt again, Andy."

Fire raced through Andy's system at the same time her thoughts seemed frozen. "Thank you, Sandy," fell from her mouth and she hung up. She looked around her festive shop like Mama would appear and give her some advice.

Last time, she'd jumped to conclusions.

Last time, she'd trusted what someone else said more than she trusted Lawrence.

Last time, her decision had cost her a year of happiness.

"Not this time," she vowed as she grabbed her keys and headed for the door. "Not this time."

The Ninth Inning

TEN MINUTES LATER, Andy sat in her car in the pancake house parking lot, seriously questioning her sanity. *What are you going to do?* she asked herself. *March in there and demand to know who he's eating with?*

She could see them through the front window. Her beautiful Lawrence and that dark-haired beauty.

Taking a deep breath, and without a plan in place, she slipped out of the car. She made her steps even as she entered the pancake house. Sandy met her eye and twitched her head toward where Andy had already seen Lawrence.

Now or never, she thought. *Help me, Lord.*

She slid into the booth next to the woman. "Lawrence," she said. She'd thought about pretending to just stumble upon them, but had dismissed the idea. She'd been aiming for truth, and he was going to get it.

"I don't know who this woman is, and I'm sure you're going to tell me. It doesn't really matter who she is. What matters is that I love you, and I trust you." Her words hit her square in the face at the same time they hit him. She found she didn't need to say anything else.

"Yeah. That's it. I love you, and I trust you. When you finish up here, come on over and you can tell me all about her." She cast a look at the woman, who wore a look of pure surprise.

Andy slid out of the booth, her heart thudding in

her chest like it was about to go belly up. She paused next to Lawrence, reached out, and grasped his fingers as he reached toward her too. Satisfied and relieved and still beyond curious, she held her head high as she left the pancake house.

Back in the safe darkness of the driveway behind her building, she let herself collapse. Without the adrenaline, Andy felt like she had no bones to support her body. But somehow, she managed to make it upstairs to her loft, half-hoping Lawrence would be waiting there for her.

Of course he wasn't.

LAWRENCE STARED AT GINA—his father's daughter from a relationship before his dad had met and married his mom. She'd been put up for adoption as an infant, had the birth certificate, his father's eyes, and Lawrence's crooked smile. Once he'd verified who she was, he'd suggested dinner. Gina claimed to want only to know where she came from, who her blood relatives were. She'd only be in Three Rivers for the night.

"You should go after her," Gina said, spearing a chunk of her whole wheat pancakes.

"I should, shouldn't I?"

The Ninth Inning

Andy's words rang in his ears. *I love you and I trust you.*

He fumbled for his wallet. "I'll leave you some money. I'm so sorry, Gina." He threw some cash on the table and stood. "You have my number?"

"I have it," she said. "Go talk to whoever that was."

Lawrence grinned. "That's my Andy." He hurried toward the exit.

"Better tell her you love her back next time!" Gina called after him.

He'd wanted to tell Andy he loved her since the day he met her. The past couple of weeks rekindling their relationship had only increased that desire. He drove too fast through town, arriving at her loft after only a few minutes. He pulled into the back driveway, directly behind her car. The lights along the top floor indicated she was home, though he knew she sometimes walked the downtown area.

He went up the back steps only to be met by a locked door. He'd come to Andy's shop after-hours enough to know where the bell was. His fingers searched for the bump on the wall, finding it after several agonizing seconds. He pressed it, satisfied when the peal resonated through the building.

Lawrence stepped back so Andy could look out the window and see him—a dance they'd perfected in the months they'd dated. Sure enough, her shadow passed by the window. Then drew nearer.

She lifted the glass and leaned her elbows on the sill. "Who are you and what do you want?"

He tilted his head back and laughed. "Andy, let me in."

She regarded him, her head cocked adorably to the side. "You never said what you wanted."

She seemed playful, yet serious at the same time. His heart raced.

"You," he said. "I want you."

She ducked back inside, and a few seconds later, the door opened. She didn't come out to meet him, but hung back in that sexy, shy way she had.

"So that woman is Gina Collins," he said as he crossed the threshold into her boutique. "She's my half-sister, put up for adoption before my dad met my mom."

Andy blinked at him. "Wow."

"Yeah." Lawrence's gaze flitted to the storeroom and back to Andy. "Care to show me your new arrivals?" He dashed off a grin.

She returned it and hipped her way into the storeroom. This time, he didn't even wait to close the door before kissing her.

"I love you, Andy," he whispered against her lips. "I've loved you forever."

Chapter Eight

Andy hurried down the stairs when she saw Lawrence's truck turn the corner. She switched on the built-in speakers and *Silent Night* filtered through the space. The grin she'd been trying to contain spilled onto her face as she unlocked the shop's door and opened it.

"Merry Christmas," she said as Lawrence appeared. She flew down the stairs and into his arms, though he had to practically throw the groceries he'd brought in order to catch her.

"Merry Christmas to you too." He chuckled and she held onto his broad shoulders even tighter.

"You sure you don't mind coming here over being at Kelly's?" Andy pulled away so she could see his face, read the lie in his eyes—if there was one.

But she couldn't find one. He kept one of her hands

in his as he bent to grab the grocery sacks he'd been carrying. "Andy, I'd rather be alone with you, trust me."

And alone they were. Just the two of them. It was the greatest Christmas present Andy had ever had. All she'd ever wanted.

"Did Santa come?" he asked as they made their way into the boutique.

She sighed and pressed further into his side. "You already know he did." And the microscopic box had been taunting her since he'd left last night.

"I know of no such thing." He'd tried to hide the fact that he'd stood in front of her Christmas tree for at least fifteen minutes, even kneeling to examine her tree skirt, exclaiming over her mother's lace work. She'd found the small, gold-wrapped box tucked into the boughs after he'd left.

"Sure." She locked the shop's door behind them, satisfied there wouldn't be any interruptions this Christmas.

"So you're sayin' you didn't get me anything for Christmas," he said as she started up the steps leading to her loft.

She turned, up a stair from him, now at the same height as him. "That's not what I said."

His hands snaked around her waist. The last few weeks of sneaking kisses in the storeroom and spending most of her awake time on Sundays with Lawrence had made her happier than she knew she could be, especially after Mama's death.

But the sting of her absence had lessened, and the loneliness that had threatened to crush Andy just a month ago had ebbed into a memory.

She leaned forward and kissed Lawrence, beyond grateful that she could, grateful that he loved her, grateful that she'd found a way to make things right between them. Overcome with emotion, she ducked her head and rested her cheek against his. "Thanks for coming."

"Mm." He turned and pressed his lips to the spot just behind her ear. "Nowhere I'd rather be."

They continued upstairs, and Lawrence hadn't taken two steps through the door when he said, "You made a ham?"

"It's Christmas," Andy said. "And it's about the only thing Mama taught me to make before she died." She went into the kitchen ahead of him. "Ham and cheesy potatoes."

"You've been holdin' out on me."

She turned and found him leaning against the couch, a delicious half-smile on his face.

"I know how to cook," Andy said. "I just don't do much of it during my busy season."

He stalked a step closer. "So you're sayin' when it's not busy, we can eat like this every Sunday?"

She shrugged, though a zing of delight pulsed through her. He came closer and closer still. "Should we eat first or open presents first?"

"Presents," Andy said. "The ham has another hour at least." She tipped her head back as he drew her into an embrace. "And it's only ten o'clock in the morning."

"Presents it is." He kissed her, and Andy thought she could lose hours to Lawrence's touch. She thanked the Lord for Lawrence's calming and comforting presence in her life at this precious time of year.

As he took her hand and led her toward the Christmas tree, Andy wondered if every holiday season could be as magical as this one had been. She hoped so.

THE ANGRY BEES that had taken up residence in Lawrence's chest buzzed louder with every step toward the Christmas tree. Andy had obviously already seen the box he'd left last night. It had taken every ounce of self-control he possessed to stop himself from giving it to her then. But he wanted it to be a true Christmas gift.

He didn't care if she got him anything, though he was sure she had. The four wrapped boxes under the

The Ninth Inning

tree hadn't been there last night, and she'd already sent gifts out to the ladies and cowboys at Three Rivers.

"So you sit here." He led her to the couch. "And I'll start." He plucked the box from the branches, his heart beating so fast he thought it might burst.

He cleared his throat, and though he'd already said all these words to Andy at some point over the last several weeks, he somehow couldn't order them now.

"I've known you were the one for me from the day we met," he said, this part of the proposal completely unplanned. "And I want to be with you for the rest of my life." He thrust the box toward her, unsure of what to say next.

She unwrapped the box and took out the jewelry container. Her eyes widened when she looked inside. "Lawrence," she breathed.

"It's an emerald," he said, gently taking the box from her fingers as he sat next to her on the couch. "A real one. For your gemstone." He couldn't get the emotion out of his voice. "And though we haven't been able to share your birthday together, when I saw this ring, I thought it would be perfect for—"

His voice stopped working completely, so he carefully removed the ring and started to slide it on her finger. Her left ring finger.

Her gaze flew to his. "Lawrence." Her voice held a note of warning.

He kept his eyes locked on hers. "I thought it would be perfect for an engagement ring." His throat felt like someone had swapped it with sand and cotton. "I love you, Andy. I want to see you everyday, not just on Sundays. Will you marry me so we can make that happen?"

His body had forgotten how to do all its involuntary functions. She didn't seem to be breathing or blinking either. "Well, now my gift is going to seem really lame," she whispered.

"Not if you say yes," he said. "You're all I need for Christmas."

With her eyes drifting closed and her leaning closer, she said, "Yes, Lawrence. Yes, I'll marry you."

Fireworks popped through his mind, bringing a smile to his lips just before he sealed their engagement with a Christmas kiss.

The End

Read on for a sneak peek at the next book in the Three Rivers Ranch Romance™ series! - **TEN DAYS IN TOWN!**

Sneak Peek! Ten Days in Town Chapter One

The dates Sandy Keller had been on hadn't been so disastrous in at least six months. Maybe longer. She'd been out with so many men, she'd lost count. Of course, she hadn't ever had to drive out to Three Rivers Ranch to pick up her date before. That was a new low.

And so was having him say the words "my girlfriend" while *she* paid for dinner.

She fumed as she pulled into the parking lot, the long drive of shame back from the ranch finally over. Sandy didn't want to return to the pancake house, where she'd have to explain to the night manager how utterly ridiculous dating in Three Rivers had become.

"Only for you," she muttered as she turned the corner and headed toward the back building. Her oasis away from everything, her condo sat around the rear of the building, giving her unprecedented views of the western range. Living on the very edge of town had its perks, she supposed.

She pressed the brake too hard, jerking her car to a stop. Someone had parked in her designated space. Again.

Muttering, she backed up and found an uncovered parking spot, eyeing the red SUV like it had done her a personal wrong. She unlocked her front door and eased into her condo like she was settling into a warm bath.

Coming home had always brought her comfort. So had cooking. She whipped out a batch of oatmeal chocolate chip cookies, slid the tray into the oven, and disappeared into her bedroom to change. She wished she could slip away from the night's horrors as easily as she shed one set of clothes and replaced them with silky pajamas.

She looked at herself in the bathroom mirror, trying to see her flaws. Oh, she had them—a lot of them—but she couldn't understand why everyone around her seemed to be able to find someone to love and she couldn't.

"No more dating anyone from the ranch," she told her reflection.

Sure, she'd been on some fun dates with some nice guys. But she hadn't made it past the third date in over a year. There had to be something wrong with her, but looking at her brown eyes and highlighted brown hair, she couldn't see it.

So, like she'd done dozens of times before, she returned to the kitchen to drown out the memories of her terrible date in ooey gooey chocolate.

The timer beeped once as she came out of her bedroom—the signal that it had been going off for a while. Her adrenaline spiked. How long had she been staring at herself in the mirror?

Thin, white smoke issued from the vents at the rear of the oven. She hurried into the kitchen, grabbed the oven mitts from the drawer, and yanked open the door.

Smoke and heat and vapor smacked her in the face. She cringed and pulled back, her stomach rioting over the loss of the cookies.

She'd barely slammed the ruined sheet of what was going to be her saving grace for the night on the stovetop when someone opened her front door.

Panic poured through her in waves, and she lifted her still oven-mitted hands like she could ward off any attack with them.

"Sandy?" a man asked.

Through the haze, Sandy made out the tall form of her brother, Hank. Relief made her sag against the peninsula. Just as quickly, she straightened and marched into the living room. "What are you doing here?"

Hank lifted his duffle bag. "We're here for the holidays." He peered at her, something he had to do to actually see her through the smoke hanging in the air. "Did you forget Ma was gettin' new floors done this week?" He gestured to someone standing behind him. "You said me and Tad could stay here."

Sandy tried to see her brother's best friend from college, but he lingered directly behind Hank. "I did say that." She stepped back. "Come on in. I haven't gotten the beds made up yet. Weren't you coming tomorrow?"

"Willow's coming in tomorrow."

Of course. Willow, Hank's bubbly, blonde girlfriend. Well, fiancé now that he'd asked her to marry him. Sandy's only comfort all these years had been that Hank hadn't been able to get married either. She hadn't been the only disappointment to her mother. But come June, she would be.

Hank stepped into the living room, finally revealing Tad. He flashed a mega watt grin that made Sandy's heart go flippity-flop and stepped forward. "Sandy, it's so good to see you again."

She stared at his outstretched hand, not quite sure if she trusted herself to shake it. Seconds stretched into awkwardness, which Hank broke by saying, "Don't you own the pancake house now? How is it possible for you to burn cookies?"

The Ninth Inning

Embarrassment flooded Sandy's cheeks, along with a healthy dose of heat. She turned away from Tad's tall frame, his intoxicating dark eyes, which still watched her, his windswept, dark chocolate-colored hair. She'd met him a few times in the past, only for a couple of minutes. But now he screamed *available!* even though she'd just sworn off dating.

You just swore off dating anyone living at the ranch, she amended as she went to open the windows in the dining room. *And Tad doesn't live out at the ranch.*

She gave herself a mental shake, a stern reminder not to be ridiculous. Tad was going to be here for ten days, not forever. And Sandy, owner of the steady and successful pancake house, was a lifetime resident of Three Rivers. The thought had never felt like such a life sentence.

Tad Jorgensen watched Sandy Keller—his best friend's little sister—slink into the dining room to open windows. He'd left the front door open, but not because he'd thought it would help clear out the gauzy smoke. But because Sandy's beauty had struck him full in the chest, rendering him slow of thought. It had been a miracle he'd managed to say hello and offer his hand to her.

She hadn't taken it, and now he focused on his fingers, thinking them covered with slime or something.

Sandy's light laugh brought Tad out of his trance. His pulse quickened when she glanced his way, and he needed to pull himself together. Fast. He'd come up with a plausible reason he could go home for Christmas with Hank this year when he'd never been able to before. Mandatory vacation.

Helicopter pilots rarely got vacation, especially in the tourist industry where Tad worked. *Used to work,* he thought as he watched Sandy and Hank banter in the kitchen. His fingers itched to touch her silky pajamas, and he reined in his thoughts.

She's your best friend's sister, he told himself. *And you're unemployed.*

Even if she had burnt the cookies, she wouldn't be interested in a helicopter pilot who was afraid to fly.

Bitterness, now becoming more and more familiar as the weeks passed, coated his throat. He had been asked to take a mandatory vacation over the holidays—usually the busiest time of the year—but it wasn't because he'd stored up too many days.

He forced his mind somewhere—anywhere—else, and the traitorous thing landed back on Sandy.

"Didn't think you'd be here," Hank said when

Tad's brain started working again. "That's why I opened the door without knocking."

"Why wouldn't I be here?" Sandy sat at her bar, her back to Tad, but he heard the false note in her voice.

"You said you had a date." Hank pinned her with an older brother look that said *Well, why aren't you out?*

Sandy's shoulders fell, and her chin dipped for half a beat. It could've been Tad's imagination, but he swore she angled her face in his direction when she said, "I'm not really into dating right now. I have the pancake house to whip into shape and...." He let her sentence hang there, and Tad wasn't sure if she didn't know how to finish it or just didn't want to in mixed company.

Hank frowned, his confusion evident. "I thought you liked—"

"Hank," she warned. "So, which of you wants my office?" She stood and faced Tad fully. Again, the subtle strength in her face, the set of her shoulders hit Tad in a way it never had before. An edge of sadness also rode in her expression, barely noticeable. In fact, Tad wondered if anyone else would be able to see it. Or if he could because the same vein of despair had been lingering with him since the beginning of

November, when he'd barely made it back to the rim of the Grand Canyon.

In many ways, he was still out there. Still lost in the wilderness. Still radioing for help.

His clients hadn't filed any complaints. Their version of what had happened painted him in a complimentary light. But everything about Tad's confidence had been shattered. He'd thought he understood his helicopter; he'd been flying over the Grand Canyon for years. But nothing had prepared him and no experience could've helped him during that fateful flight.

"Tad?" Sandy stood in front of him now, but he hadn't seen her move.

"I'll take the office," Tad said. "Sure." He glanced left and right, seeing only one door to the right of the kitchen. That would be her room. On the left, an arched doorway revealed a hall branching in both directions, with a closed door at the junction. He stepped that way.

"I can set up my own bed. Or sleep on the couch. The floor. Whatever." He didn't want to add to Sandy's load. She looked and sounded a bit worn down.

His attention came back to her when she said, "Let me clean up in there first," with a tremor of trepidation in her tone.

He paused upon entering the hall. Her office obvi-

The Ninth Inning

ously existed to his right, but he didn't want to enter it unless she approved. "Sure. Is this the bathroom?"

"Yeah." Sandy squeezed behind him and entered the office. "I'll just be a minute." She closed the door, that panicked edge in her eye kicking Tad's pulse into a new gear.

He turned away, frustrated with himself. He could not be attracted to Hank's little sister, even if she was twenty-seven years old. Tad joined Hank in the kitchen, where he stood at the sink, staring out the window.

"Three Rivers," he said, though darkness had fallen an hour ago and not much could be seen.

"So much sky," Hank added, and Tad appreciated being able to see something in a way Las Vegas had never allowed. He could see the stars without straining. Coming into town, Tad had felt the smallness of it, and something about it sang to his soul.

He hadn't told anyone about the flight that had almost ended his life, and had definitely stalled his career.

"So what's here?" he asked Hank.

Hank shrugged and turned away from the window. "Small town stuff." He spoke as if small towns had nothing to offer. But Tad craved the tranquility and peace of a place like Three Rivers. Somewhere where no one knew him, no one thought of him as a helicopter pilot, no one assumed anything about him.

Stay, he thought, and the feeling spread through him slowly, like honey dripping from the hive. Tad closed his eyes and drank in the peace emanating from the very air in Three Rivers.

He was going to stay—and not just for the ten days with Hank. But for good.

His decision made, and approved of by the Lord, Tad couldn't wait to spend some time alone. Because now he needed to figure out what he could do in Three Rivers to make a living.

* * *

Look for TEN DAYS IN TOWN by scanning the QR code below!

Second Chance Ranch: A Three Rivers Ranch Romance™ (Book 1): After his deployment, injured and discharged Major Squire Ackerman returns to Three Rivers Ranch, wanting to forgive Kelly for ignoring him a decade ago. He'd like to provide the stable life she needs, but with old wounds opening and a ranch on the brink of financial collapse, it will take patience and faith to make their second chance possible.

Third Time's the Charm: A Three Rivers Ranch Romance™ (Book 2): First Lieutenant Peter Marshall has a truckload of debt and no way to provide for a family, but Chelsea helps him see past all the obstacles, all the scars. With so many unknowns, can Pete and Chelsea develop the love, acceptance, and faith needed to find their happily ever after?

Fourth and Long: A Three Rivers Ranch Romance™ (Book 3): Commander Brett Murphy goes to Three Rivers Ranch to find some rest and relaxation with his Army buddies. Having his ex-wife show up with a seven-year-old she claims is his son is anything but the R&R he craves. Kate needs to make amends, and Brett needs to find forgiveness, but are they too late to find their happily ever after?

Fifth Generation Cowboy: A Three Rivers Ranch Romance™ (Book 4): Tom Lovell has watched his friends find their true happiness on Three Rivers Ranch, but everywhere he looks, he only sees friends. Rose Reyes has been bringing her daughter out to the ranch for equine therapy for months, but it doesn't seem to be working. Her challenges with Mari are just as frustrating as ever. Could Tom be exactly what Rose needs? Can he remove his friendship blinders and find love with someone who's been right in front of him all this time?

**Sixth Street Love Affair: A Three Rivers Ranch Romance™ (Book 5):** After losing his wife a few years back, Garth Ahlstrom thinks he's ready for a second chance at love. But Juliette Thompson has a secret that could destroy their budding relationship. Can they find the strength, patience, and faith to make things work?

The Seventh Sergeant: A Three Rivers Ranch Romance™ (Book 6): Life has finally started to settle down for Sergeant Reese Sanders after his devastating injury overseas. Discharged from the Army and now with a good job at Courage Reins, he's finally found happiness—until a horrific fall puts him right back where he was years ago: Injured and depressed. Carly Watters, Reese's new veteran care coordinator, dislikes small towns almost as much as she loathes cowboys. But she finds herself faced with both when she gets assigned to Reese's case. Do they have the humility and faith to make their relationship more than professional?

Eight Second Ride: A Three Rivers Ranch Romance™ (Book 7): Ethan Greene loves his work at Three Rivers Ranch, but he can't seem to find the right woman to settle down with. When sassy yet vulnerable Brynn Bowman shows up at the ranch to recruit him back to the rodeo circuit, he takes a different approach with the barrel racing champion. His patience and newfound faith pay off when a friendship--and more--starts with Brynn. But she wants out of the rodeo circuit right when Ethan wants to rejoin. Can they find the path God wants them to take and still stay together?

The Ninth Inning: A Three Rivers Ranch Romance™ (Book 8): The Christmas season has never felt like such a burden to boutique owner Andrea Larsen. But with Mama gone and the holidays upon her, Andy finds herself wishing she hadn't been so quick to judge her former boyfriend, cowboy Lawrence Collins. Well, Lawrence hasn't forgotten about Andy either, and he devises a plan to get her out to the ranch so they can reconnect. Do they have the faith and humility to patch things up and start a new relationship?

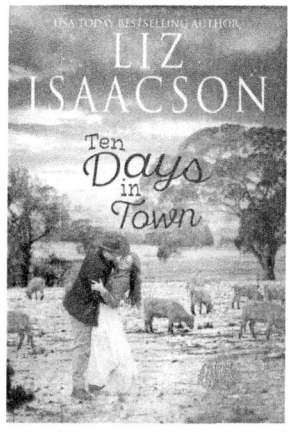

Ten Days in Town: A Three Rivers Ranch Romance™ (Book 9): Sandy Keller is tired of the dating scene in Three Rivers. Though she owns the pancake house, she's looking for a fresh start, which means an escape from the town where she grew up. When her older brother's best friend, Tad Jorgensen, comes to town for the holidays, it is a balm to his weary soul. A helicopter tour guide who experienced a near-death experience, he's looking to start over too--but in Three Rivers. Can Sandy and Tad navigate their troubles to find the path God wants them to take--and discover true love--in only ten days?

Eleven Year Reunion: A Three Rivers Ranch Romance™ (Book 10): Pastry chef extraordinaire, Grace Lewis has moved to Three Rivers to help Heidi Ackerman open a bakery in Three Rivers. Grace relishes the idea of starting over in a town where no one knows about her failed cupcakery. She doesn't expect to run into her old high school boyfriend, Jonathan Carver. A carpenter working at Three Rivers Ranch, Jon's in town against his will. But with Grace now on the scene, Jon's thinking life in Three Rivers is suddenly looking up. But with her focus on baking and his disdain for small towns, can they make their eleven year reunion stick?

The Twelfth Town: A Three Rivers Ranch Romance™ (Book 11): Newscaster Taryn Tucker has had enough of life on-screen. She's bounced from town to town before arriving in Three Rivers, completely alone and completely anonymous--just the way she now likes it. She takes a job cleaning at Three Rivers Ranch, hoping for a chance to figure out who she is and where God wants her. When she meets happy-go-lucky cowhand Kenny Stockton, she doesn't expect sparks to fly. Kenny's always been "the best friend" for his female friends, but the pull between him and Taryn can't be denied. Will they have the courage and faith necessary to make their opposite worlds mesh?

Lucky Number Thirteen: A Three Rivers Ranch Romance™ (Book 12): Tanner Wolf, a rodeo champion ten times over, is excited to be riding in Three Rivers for the first time since he left his philandering ways and found religion. Seeing his old friends Ethan and Brynn is therapuetic--until a terrible accident lands him in the hospital. With his rodeo career over, Tanner thinks maybe he'll stay in town--and it's not just because his nurse, Summer Hamblin, is the prettiest woman he's ever met. But Summer's the queen of first dates, and as she looks for a way to make a relationship with the transient rodeo star work Summer's not sure she has the fortitude to go on a second date. Can they find love among the tragedy?

The Curse of February Fourteenth: A Three Rivers Ranch Romance™ (Book 13): Cal Hodgkins, cowboy veterinarian at Bowman's Breeds, isn't planning to meet anyone at the masked dance in small-town Three Rivers. He just wants to get his bachelor friends off his back and sit on the sidelines to drink his punch. But when he sees a woman dressed in gorgeous butterfly wings and cowgirl boots with blue stitching, he's smitten. Too bad she runs away from the dance before he can get her name, leaving only her boot behind...

Fifteen Minutes of Fame: A Three Rivers Ranch Romance™ (Book 14): Navy Richards is thirty-five years of tired—tired of dating the same men, working a demanding job, and getting her heart broken over and over again. Her aunt has always spoken highly of the matchmaker in Three Rivers, Texas, so she takes a six-month sabbatical from her high-stress job as a pediatric nurse, hops on a bus, and meets with the matchmaker. Then she meets Gavin Redd. He's handsome, he's hardworking, and he's a cowboy. But is he an Aquarius too? Navy's not making a move until she knows for sure...

Sixteen Steps to Fall in Love: A Three Rivers Ranch Romance™ (Book 15): A chance encounter at a dog park sheds new light on the tall, talented Boone that Nicole can't ignore. As they get to know each other better and start to dig into each other's past, Nicole is the one who wants to run. This time from her growing admiration and attachment to Boone. From her aging parents. From herself.

But Boone feels the attraction between them too, and he decides he's tired of running and ready to make Three Rivers his permanent home. **Can Boone and Nicole use their faith to overcome their differences and find a happily-ever-after together?**

The Sleigh on Seventeenth Street: A Three Rivers Ranch Romance™ (Book 16): A cowboy with skills as an electrician tries a relationship with a down-on-her luck plumber. Can Dylan and Camila make water and electricity play nicely together this Christmas season? Or will they get shocked as they try to make their relationship work?

The First Lady of Three Rivers Ranch: A Three Rivers Ranch Romance™ (Book 17): Heidi Duffin has been dreaming about opening her own bakery since she was thirteen years old. She scrimped and saved for years to afford baking and pastry school in San Francisco. And now she only has one year left before she's a certified pastry chef. Frank Ackerman's father has recently retired, and he's taken over the largest cattle ranch in the Texas Panhandle. A horseman through and through, he's also nearing thirty-one and looking for someone to bring love and joy to a homestead that's been dominated by men for a decade. But when he convinces Heidi to come clean the cowboy cabins, she changes all that. But the siren's call of a bakery is still loud in Heidi's ears, even if she's also seeing a future with Frank. Can she rely on her faith in ways she's never had to before or will their relationship end when summer does?

Second Generation in Three Rivers Romance™ Series

Step back into the heartwarming small Texas town of Three Rivers! This beloved town has captured the hearts of 2.5 million readers and caught the eye of Sony Pictures, and now a new generation of cowboys and cowgirls is ready to take center stage. Scan the QR code below with your phone to check out this new series!

1. The Cowboy Who Came Home - featuring Squire's son, Finn from SECOND CHANCE RANCH!

Seven Sons Ranch in Three Rivers Romance™ Series

Meet the cowboy billionaire brothers at Seven Sons Ranch! Scan the QR code below with your phone to check out this complete series.

1. Rhett's Make-Believe Marriage
2. Tripp's Trivial Tie
3. Liam's Invented I-Do
4. Jeremiah's Bogus Bride
5. Wyatt's Pretend Pledge
6. Skyler's Wanna-Be Wife
7. Micah's Mock Matrimony
8. Gideon's Precious Penny

Shiloh Ridge Ranch in Three Rivers Romance™ Series

Meet the cowboy billionaires in the southern hills outside of Three Rivers! Scan the QR code below with your phone to check out this complete series.

1. The Mechanics of Mistletoe
2. The Horsepower of the Holiday
3. The Construction of Cheer
4. The Secret of Santa
5. The Gift of Gingerbread
6. The Harmony of Holly
7. The Chemistry of Christmas
8. The Delivery of Decor
9. The Blessing of Babies
10. The Networking of the Nativity
11. The Wrangling of the Wreath
12. The Hope of Her Heart

About Liz

Liz Isaacson writes inspirational romance, usually set in Texas, or Wyoming, or anywhere else horses and cowboys exist. She lives in Utah, where she writes full-time, takes her two dogs to the park everyday, and eats a lot of veggies while writing. Find all of her books on her website at feelgoodfictionbooks.com.

Printed in Great Britain
by Amazon